DEATH HUNT

A BREED THRILLER

CAMERON CURTIS

INKUBATOR
BOOKS

Published by Inkubator Books
www.inkubatorbooks.com

Copyright © 2025 by Cameron Curtis

Cameron Curtis has asserted his right to be identified as the author of this work.

ISBN (eBook): 978-1-83756-539-9
ISBN (Paperback): 978-1-83756-540-5

DEATH HUNT is a work of fiction. People, places, events, and situations are the product of the author's imagination. Any resemblance to actual persons, living or dead is entirely coincidental.

No part of this book may be reproduced, stored in any retrieval system, or transmitted by any means without the prior written permission of the publisher.

Bourbon Street

Miriam Winslet House

Palace Cafe

St. Charles Streetcar

Cruelty has a Human Heart
And Jealousy a Human Face
Terror the Human Form Divine
And Secrecy, the Human Dress

The Human Dress, is forged Iron.
The Human Form, a fiery Forge.
The Human Face, a Furnace seal'd
The Human Heart, its hungry Gorge.

—William Blake, "A Divine Image" 1789

front door and elbow their way past the lineup. The others rush toward the back of the building.

"Come on." I grab Ellie by the arm and hurry through the swinging door into the kitchen.

The interior is steamy, filled with the smell of greasy food. Kitchen staff look up in shock. I push Ellie ahead.

Kitchens are dangerous places. The first man comes through the door. I snatch a cleaver from a chopping block. Hurl it with all my strength, bury it in the man's face. The blade crosses the T from between his eyebrows down the bridge of his nose. The man behind shoves him out of the way and throws himself at me.

There's a big commercial oven to my right. The heavy door is ajar, and I don't feel heat coming from the interior. I grasp the edge of the frame and swing the oven door into the man's face. There's a crunch, and blood splashes across the cracked window. The man rocks back on his heels.

I grab the front of the man's shirt, twist it in my fist, hold him up like a hundred-and-sixty-pound rag doll. His eyes are glassy, his face a crimson mask from the nose down. I let go. Before he falls, I smash the oven door into his face a second time. Featureless, bone structure crushed beyond recognition, he crumples like an empty suit of clothes.

Turn. Ellie's standing with one eye on me and the other on the back door. "Breed!"

I take Ellie by the hand and make for the exit. Kitchen workers scatter in all directions. I grab the handle and jerk the door open. Run into the two men who stayed outside.

I grab the first man by the lapels. He looks at me with terrified eyes. I jerk him close and butt him. It's like hitting him in the face with a ten-pound bowling ball. His eyes roll back in their sockets.

No guns. The guy in the restaurant had one for intimidation. But they know this is the French Quarter, and shots will attract police. There might even be plainclothes officers around.

I push the first man aside. His buddy jabs with his left fist. Son of a bitch is wearing brass knuckles. I dodge, kick the inside of his right knee with the side of my boot. There's a crack, and the man goes down with a shriek. Brass knucks don't do you much good on the ground. I shift my weight and use his face for soccer practice.

The guy's resilient. Tries to struggle back to his feet. I grab the circular lid from a metal garbage can. The stale smell of restaurant waste spills into the air. Holding the lid with both hands, I bring the flat side down on the guy's head. Once, twice. He slumps to one knee. The metal of the lid's bent. I shift my grip so I'm holding it one-handed. Smash the edge against the side of his head at the level of his ear. There's a clang, and the man falls on his side. He looks up at me, and I smash the edge against his face again and again. Burst his nose, knock in his front teeth, slash it across his eyes. He raises a hand to ward off the blows, and I step on his wrist to hold him down. Pound his face until he lies still.

I step back, toss the lid aside. The misshapen lump of metal clangs on the pavement.

There's no one in the alley, no one emerging from the restaurant. I take Ellie by the arm and guide her around the corner to Iberville Street.

New Orleans' planners tried to lay out the city in blocks with straight streets, much like Paris. Unfortunately, the Mississippi is far more sinuous than the Seine. The streets this side of the Quarter run parallel to the river, then dogleg around its curve. Iberville Street runs straight north by west, away from my hotel.

Pedestrian traffic on Iberville is light. I look each way, lead Ellie northwest. We pass an ugly concrete parkade on our left. The streets of New Orleans are narrow. The pavement is cracked and uneven. Somehow, streets in the Quarter look dirty even after cleaning. Everything looks a little dingy in daylight. Only when darkness falls does the Quarter come into its own—fun, sexy, rowdy and dangerous.

"How did those men find you?" I ask.

"They must have been watching my hotel," Ellie says. "I didn't see them follow me."

"Where's your hotel?"

"Chartres Street, the other side of Jackson Square."

"You're not going back there," I tell her. "Ever."

"Where are we going?"

"My hotel. It's on Royal Street, but I want us to get lost in a crowd first."

We hurry past Chartres and Royal, turn east on Bourbon. It's everything one expects from the French Quarter. The sun's going down, and people flow both ways over the street. They're drinking Hurricanes—rum and fruit juice—from open paper cups. An eclectic mix of jazz, zydeco and pounding club music filters from the bars and clubs. Gay laughter comes from second-floor balconies. Men and women lean against the intricate wrought-iron rails, drinking and smoking.

A scantily dressed blond woman sits on a stool at the entrance to a club. The walls strain against a throbbing bass. She's displaying bare legs that stretch to Canada. Ellie stares at a snake draped over her shoulders. The creature's body is as thick as my forearm, coiled in her lap. Its head hangs between her heavy breasts.

The woman addresses me. "Hey, hon, where ya at?"

I blow her a kiss, guide Ellie past.

"Like them young?" The woman's smile is lascivious. "Me too. We could have fun, us and you."

Snake and woman watch us walk past. The woman's reptilian tongue flicks across her lips.

My arm is around Ellie's shoulders. She clutches my waist and we shiver together.

People don't call this city The Big Easy for nothing.

2

DAY ONE - FRENCH QUARTER, 1900 HRS

The Jean Lafitte is a cozy three-star hotel on Royal Street. It's a converted Spanish colonial. Two stories. After the fire of 1794, laws were passed that all construction should be of brick. There's a flagstone *porte cochère*—a carriageway that leads to a central courtyard and circular fountain. The ground floor is surrounded by a narrow loggia.

Hanging baskets dripping ferns and brightly colored flowers adorn the second-floor balconies. The ferns stretch from the wrought-iron rails to the flagstones of the courtyard below. The hotel office is in front, to the left. To the right, a small coffee shop.

I book a second room on the second floor, the side opposite mine. Use my name. I introduce Ellie to the middle-aged desk clerk as my niece, my sister's daughter. If those men followed her from her hotel, they'll have the name she used to check in. How they found her hotel in the first place is problematic.

We're alone in the coffee shop. The Lafitte is family

owned and managed. The desk clerk's husband takes our orders. Our dinner is hardly Louisiana cuisine—roast turkey, stuffing, and baked potatoes. We order mugs of ice-cold beer.

"You're not old enough to drink," I tell her.

Ellie fixes me with an amused stare. "I'm old enough for a *lot* of things. My ID says so."

I bet.

"You don't *look* twenty-one."

Ellie shrugs. "It's dark. No one gives a shit."

I decide to park it. "Who *were* those men?"

"I don't know. They're with the bunch who took my sister."

"Okay, let's pick up where we left off. Before we were so rudely interrupted."

"Breed, I've lost count of the badasses you've killed. I think you may have *anger* issues."

I frown, and Ellie smiles mischievously. "The thing with the straw was pretty cool," she says. "How does that work?"

"Your thumb traps air in the straw," I tell her. "Makes it stiff as a steel rod."

"I bet you're pretty good with a stiff rod."

I roll my eyes. "This is your dime. Tell me about your sister."

She does.

A YEAR AGO, Ellie and I occupied separate hospital rooms across the hall from each other. Neither of us was badly wounded. Ellie's shoulder wound had been stitched up. She was loaded with antibiotics, and she was healing.

Ellie had bigger problems. Stein came to visit her one evening.

"It's good to see you," Ellie said, "but aren't visiting hours over?"

"I can do anything I want." Stein tossed her hair. "I'm the CIA."

I've known Anya Stein for four years. She's Radcliffe and Harvard Law. Former FBI, now CIA, "the Company." Her father is a private equity billionaire on Wall Street. Well connected, but she earned her position the hard way. Took calculated risks with her career, went into the field with the Ground Branch, SEALs and Delta Force. I've seen her in action.

You wouldn't know it to look at her. Thin, dark haired, attractive. Carries a SIG P226 Legion in a cross-draw holster. She swims or runs an hour a day. We've got a thing for each other but have never acted on it. Let's just say we're more than a little conflicted.

"You have an issue," Stein said. "Fortunately, I can help."

Ellie waved Stein to a guest chair by the hospital bed. Stein, dressed in her signature black suit jacket, skirt and flat-heeled shoes, sat next to Ellie. The bed smelled of freshly laundered hospital linen.

"The hospital is required, by law, to report cases like yours to the Office of Children and Family Services," Stein told her. "You have no last name, which makes you a Jane Doe. I've told the hospital the government will pay all your bills, but the OCFS has to get involved. They're sending a case worker to see you first thing tomorrow."

Ellie crossed her arms and narrowed her eyes. "I'm not talking to them."

"They have to investigate your family circumstances.

Make decisions about where you should live. Schooling is an issue. It might make sense to take you home, or put you up in a shelter."

"I'm leaving the hospital tonight." Ellie's mind raced. "I'm going back to my place. They'll never find me."

"You could, but you need follow-up care for that wound. It's not serious, but it could get infected."

"I don't have a choice."

"Yes, you do." Stein leaned forward and her eyes searched Ellie's. "Want to hear it?"

"I'm listening."

Stein's eyes glittered. "The Company is not supposed to get involved in domestic matters, but I have a certain amount of influence with the FBI and the Department of Justice. I could arrange for you to enter a kind of informal witness protection program."

"I'm not a witness."

"That's why it's informal."

"How does it work?"

"I'll assign you a handler. One of my people. We'll arrange a new identity for you. Identity papers, whatever you need. We'll get you money to start out. Find you a job anywhere you want to live. You'll stay at a safe house in New York while we arrange things. We'll have Company doctors take care of you until we're sure you're one hundred percent."

Ellie frowned. "What do I have to do for all this?"

"Let's say you've done enough. Your country owes you."

It sounded too good to be true, but Ellie figured she could handle it. Ellie could handle anything. She said yes.

Stein's informal "witness protection program" was unconventional. Everything Stein did was unconventional.

Ellie's handler, Warren, was a good-looking young man with a New England accent. His blond hair was perfectly combed, and he wore a Brooks Brothers suit. Ellie saw the butt of a pistol tucked into a holster at his hip.

Warren asked her an endless series of questions and took notes. Ellie got the feeling he was asking her questions from batteries designed to assess mental stability, capacity to function in society and make decisions.

"If you could live anywhere, what kinds of things would you like to see?"

"Someplace bright," Ellie said. "Someplace warm. I need to finish school."

"What kind of people do you want to be around?"

Ellie answered without hesitation. "People who mind their own business."

Warren smiled. "That can be arranged. Let's say much of that is up to you."

"I can make *anyone* avoid me." Ellie gave Warren a wicked smile. "*Or like me.*"

No fifteen-year-old girl should be able to smile like that. Warren looked pleased.

Ellie raised an index finger. "Can I move if I don't like the place?"

"Of course. AD Stein wants you to be comfortable."

That was the first time Ellie heard Stein addressed by her formal title. She knew Stein was wealthy, competent and respected. Now she realized she was associating with a woman who wielded real power.

Living underground for two years had made Ellie a stranger to the sun. She settled in Pensacola, on the Florida panhandle. Warren arranged an apartment for her in West Pensacola, on the way to Perdido. Found her a job in the public library. Arranged for her to study high school equivalence at a local college, much of it online.

Ellie's identities were unconventional. Not at all what Ellie imagined witness protection to be. Stein arranged for Ellie to have three identities, three different names, three different passports and three matching driver's licenses. She went by Mary Louise Kennan, but she had two more backup personas locked in a safe-deposit box at the local bank. She had bank accounts and credit cards in all three names.

As Ellie described Stein's arrangements, I realized Stein had set Ellie up as some kind of operator. An asset to be kept in Stein's pocket for the day she might be needed. Nothing urgent on the burner, mind you. Just someone to hold back for contingencies. Ellie was just the kind of intelligent, resourceful girl Stein could use.

The thought of Stein using Ellie made me angry, but it was obvious that Ellie knew she was being set up. *Everybody uses everybody*, Ellie thought. *Stein can help me get what I want.*

Ellie wanted to be reunited with her sister.

FOUR YEARS EARLIER, Ellie was eleven.

"Goddamnit, Regan, dinner's cold."

Her father's voice boomed through the confines of their four-bedroom house. It was in a nice, middle-class neighborhood in Albany, New York. Clean streets, flower beds, and bicycles on lawns. Ellie and her sister, Rowan, had separate rooms on the ground floor. Their parents had the second floor to themselves.

Ellie's father was a senior manager at the post office, and he had to commute every day.

"You're late," her mother yelled back. "Chuck it in the microwave."

Ellie stared at her father in his postal service uniform. There were sweat stains under his arms and around his collar. She smelled liquor in the air. It wasn't her imagination. Her father and 'the boys' drank every day after work, and most nights. Paydays he didn't come home. The managers were a fraternity exclusive to themselves.

He was a big man. Lettered in baseball and proud of it. Still played with the boys on weekends. Tanned by the sun. It was impossible to miss that extra bit of color in his face... from alcohol that percolated through his system. The stink of rotgut and sweat reeked from his clothing.

"Don't talk to me like that!"

Ellie was always apprehensive when her father got home, never knew how he would act. He was in an ugly state. She looked out the window. The family station wagon sat in the driveway, intact. By some miracle, he'd made it home.

There were good memories in that wagon. She rode in back, her mother and father in front, on the way to the park. Later, when Rowan came along, they made a foursome.

No good memories were worth the bad days. Ellie imagined the car, with her father in it, smashed on the freeway.

The living room was as cozy as her mother could make it. A couch with round fluffy pillows. A vase of orange tulips on the coffee table. Pictures of family hung on the walls. Ellie on a tricycle, aged four.

"You're drunk again! Damn, Clay... one day you *will* kill yourself."

Her father stripped off his jacket, laid it on the back of a chair at the dining table. "Regan, warm up my dinner."

"I said... warm it yourself."

Like an angry rattler, her father turned, swept a plate from the table, and flung it across the room. The plate turned once in the air. Scattered mashed potatoes, peas, and slices of roast beef everywhere. Onto her mother's clothes, onto her face. The edge of the plate glanced off the crown of her head.

Ellie gasped. Couldn't believe her mother was unhurt.

"Bastard," her mother screamed. "Drunken bastard!"

Her father had huge fists. She remembered she couldn't close two hands around his forearm. His biceps rippled under his shirt.

With a hard left jab, he punched her mother in the face.

Ellie's mother's head jerked. She was a strong woman, but her whole body dropped like the blow cut her legs from under her.

With a loud thud, her ass hit the floor. She fell sitting up, legs splayed. Her hands were spread on either side to support her weight. Blood trickled from her nose and dripped from her chin. Green peas and grains of yellow corn littered her hair. There was gravy on the front of her dress.

"No!" Ellie leaped forward to drag her father away from her.

Twisting from his hips, her father threw her off and sent her sprawling. All skinny arms and legs, Ellie thudded against a side table. A lamp crashed to the floor.

Ellie's fall and the crash of the lamp, woke her mother

from her stupor. She fought her way back to her feet. "Ellie, go to your room."

Her father's fist twisted in her mother's hair. Pain on her face, the bleeding woman lifted her arms to clutch at that thick wrist.

He held her there, dangling by her hair, and punched her in the face again.

And again.

Rowan stood in the doorway to her bedroom. Stared at the scene.

Ellie rushed to her little sister's side, drew the eight-year-old into the bedroom, slammed the door.

Through the thin wooden barrier, the girls heard another blow. It had a different quality, like their dad had punched a mattress. An explosion of air from a bag. They heard their mother coughing and wheezing.

Another crash.

More blows.

The girls hugged each other and crouched behind the door. Rowan began to cry quietly, burying her face against Ellie.

Hide. Run. Fly.

Where?

Ellie's phone was in her room. "Ro, where's your phone?"

They'd bought Rowan a phone only that year. So their mother could reach her at school. Rowan only used it with their mom and Ellie.

Tears running down her cheeks, Rowan stared at Ellie.

"Where, Ro? Where?"

Rowan blinked away tears, pointed at her bed. "Under the pillow."

Ellie threw the pillow aside, grabbed the phone. "Unlock it, Ro. *Do it.*"

It took three tries, Rowan's fingers were trembling so much, but she unlocked the phone. Ellie called 911. Called the police. The lady on the other end asked endless questions. "What's your name, hon? What's your address? Does your father have a gun? Does he have a knife?"

The woman's questions were taking forever.

"Get them over here," Ellie spat into the phone. "He's killing her!"

"They're coming, hon. Don't hang up."

"Hurry!"

There was a knock on the front door.

Ellie's father bellowed, "Who the fuck is that?"

"Police. Open up, please."

"Go away!"

Ellie grabbed Rowan by the shoulders. "Stay here. Don't come out."

Without waiting for an answer, Ellie rushed into the living room. The dining room and kitchen were a disaster area. Her mother was sprawled on the floor, and her father was standing over her. Ellie ran to the front door, turned the bolt, and jerked it open.

Found herself staring at two police officers. Sharply pressed blue uniforms. Short-sleeved shirts open at the collar over white T-shirts. Gold badges on their chests. Pistol belts with black semi-automatics, mace, Tasers and handcuffs. She noticed their holsters were open and their hands were on the butts. They'd run into druggies with knives and guns too many times to take chances. Cops got knifed and shot every day dealing with domestic altercations.

Ellie pointed at her father and yelled, "Stop him!"

The neighbors came out to watch the cops put her father on the ground, cuff him, and haul him away to sleep it off. Her mother refused to press charges. Embarrassed, she made Ellie promise not to call the police again.

A month later, her father came home drunk and blackened her mother's eyes. Ellie felt like she was watching the same movie. Her father had her mother up against the wall and was slapping her. Forehand, backhand. Forehand, backhand. Her mother's hair flew with every blow.

"Stop it!" Ellie screamed.

Her father went on slapping her mother.

"Stop it, or I'll call the police!" Ellie held up her phone.

"No, Ellie!" Her mother's eyes were unfocused, but she managed to get the words out. "You promised."

Her father had stopped the beating to turn and look at her. Their eyes locked for a long moment. Silently, he turned away and hit her mother again.

Ellie's temples throbbed with blood. She turned and walked past Rowan. Went to the living room closet and jerked it open. Inside, her father's baseball bat was leaning against the wall. Ellie picked up the Louisville Slugger and gripped it with both hands. Walked to her father. He had his arm raised to strike her mother, and she swung the bat into his ribs like she was chopping down a tree.

There was a mighty thud. Her father cried out, turned around with a snarl, clutching his side. She raised the bat over her head and tried to bring it down on his head. He dodged, and the blow fell on his shoulder and chest. Snapped his left collar bone. With a howl, he fell to the floor.

Ellie kept her promise not to call the police.

She called an ambulance.

NOT LONG AFTER Ellie turned twelve, he came to her room. She fought, and he punched her in the ribs. Forced himself on her. She felt like she had been stabbed in the belly. Ellie was shocked by the pain and violence of the attack but didn't stop fighting. Resistance urged him on. Only when her father had gathered himself and stumbled out of her room did she notice the blood on her thighs and sheets. When he had left, Ellie rolled out of bed and crumpled to the floor. Staggered to the bathroom and washed. She wanted to cry but forced herself to think.

Ellie stole all the money she could from the house, took anything of value she could sell, and ran away. Before leaving, she went to Rowan and promised to come back for her. Told her sister she would call from a different phone number so their parents wouldn't know it was her. Ellie began the journey that led her to the underground in New York City. She learned to survive, but she was working against a ticking clock.

That ticking clock was Rowan. She was nine when Ellie ran away from home. Ellie feared that by the time her little sister turned twelve, their father would turn on her too. That gave Ellie three years. Her plan was to save money, find a place to live, and send for Rowan.

Ellie lived by her wits. Learned to read people, manipulate situations. There were times Ellie hated herself, but Rowan was her reason to keep going. The girls stayed in touch by email and messaging apps. Ellie was desperate to rescue her sister, but couldn't make things happen fast enough.

When Ellie ran into Breed and Stein in the tunnels, she was fifteen and Rowan was twelve. She was out of time.

Breed and Stein seemed like good people. Stein was filthy rich, ambitious and cunning. But she was committed to a cause higher than herself. Breed was different. Ellie crushed on him right away. He was quiet, gallant and brave. The kind of man to whom the word "honor" meant keeping one's word and doing the right thing. Breed and Stein were people Ellie felt she could look up to.

When Stein offered her protection, Ellie accepted the deal. It would help her save Rowan. And it would keep a tenuous connection between herself and her new friends. Because whatever else Ellie was, she was lonely.

Ellie was about set up in Pensacola, ready to send for Rowan, when she got a call at five o'clock in the morning. Rowan was hysterical—the worst had happened. She was calling from a McDonald's in downtown Albany. She had nothing but her phone and the clothes on her back.

"Ellie... what... are... we going to... *do*?" Rowan spoke between sobs. Her voice was quivering.

"Ro, you're coming to me, right now."

"Ellie, I have to go to the police."

"What? No. You can't."

"There's blood on my bed. Blood in the bathroom. The police will know what to do."

"The police will take you away from Mom and Dad and put you somewhere you and I can never be together. Is that what you want?"

Rowan's voice cracked. "No! But I don't have any money. I don't know where to go."

Ellie spoke slowly and deliberately. She wanted her own calm to rub off on Rowan. "You are coming to me. Do exactly what I tell you. Everything will be fine."

If they were lucky, their parents were still asleep and hadn't reported Rowan missing. The police would be sure to cruise the streets, check the airport and bus terminal. There wasn't a lot of time.

Ellie checked the Greyhound routes. There was nothing direct from Albany to Pensacola. Pensacola's location on the Gulf Coast, at the center of the panhandle, made it hard to reach from the north. The fastest routes were straight down to New Orleans to the west, or Jacksonville to the east. Then transfer onto a bus to Pensacola.

They had to get Rowan out of town fast. The first bus out of Albany was headed to New Orleans. Ellie bought the ticket online and emailed the ticket to Rowan.

The trip would take well over a day. How long would it take for Rowan to be reported missing? How long would it take for a girl matching her description to be identified at the bus station? It would take time. In the old days, you rocked up to the ticket counter and bought your ticket. The ticket vendor would remember you. To use an emailed ticket, you went straight to the bus and showed it on your phone.

Warren had reviewed internet protocols with Ellie. Made sure her traffic was untraceable. She was fitted with a Company VPN that ensured her security. The police would check all the tickets purchased that morning, but would have no way to tell exactly which one Rowan used.

Most likely, they would identify the buses that left before the girl was reported missing. Then they would try to catch the buses at their stops. Find out if a girl matching Rowan's description boarded or got off.

Rowan had to get to New Orleans, then transfer to a bus to Jacksonville. It would travel along the Gulf Coast. One stop at Mobile, and they'd be together.

The girls sweated every stop. Rowan watched the passing traffic for police cars. At the bus stations she wouldn't leave the bus. Quivered at the thought of police boarding and checking the passengers.

She made it to New Orleans before the plan unraveled.

Rowan got off the bus to wait for her transfer. It was a three-hour stop. She found a bench in a corner of the waiting area. Surrounded by rows of lockers, their doors painted bright red. The station served both Greyhound and Amtrak. Buses and trains.

She was thirteen years old, feeling very small and frightened. Rowan's hands shook. Ellie messaged her to stay calm.

A police cruiser pulled up outside the station. Rowan knew she would be spotted if she stayed where she was. She got up and walked out to the buses. Stepped between the long coaches to conceal herself from the police in the station's main hall. Her nose wrinkled at the stench of grease and diesel fumes.

Rowan hurried past lines of passengers. Left the boarding area and walked onto the street. To her horror, the tall city buildings looked like they were a mile away. She faced a broad, open parking lot with no place to hide. She didn't know which direction to turn.

Across from the parking lot was a multilevel parking

arcade. Why would they build a parkade next to a parking lot? It didn't matter. The point was, if she could get to the parkade, she could lose herself. Heart pounding, she walked straight across the parking lot, weaving between parked cars as much as she could.

When she reached the parkade, she stepped into its cool, shadowy interior and sat down. Peered around the corner and looked back at the station. No one was following her. She took out her phone and called Ellie.

"The bus on which you arrived," Ellie said. "Was it still there when you saw the police?"

"I don't remember." Rowan was flustered. "Why?"

"Because if it was still there, the police can speak to the driver. Would he remember you?"

"I don't know," Rowan said. "I didn't speak to him."

"Were you the only kid on the bus?"

"Yes."

"He'll remember you."

"I can't remember if the bus was still there."

"We have to assume that it was." Ellie was thinking fast. "You can't catch your transfer to Pensacola. You have to stay in New Orleans for a while until they get tired of looking for you."

Rowan's voice rose in pitch. "How long will that be?"

"Calm down. Hundreds of kids run away every day. They disappear, and so will you. You need to find a place to stay for a few days."

"I don't know *anything* about this city."

"Sit tight, Ro," Ellie told her. "Leave it to me."

Ellie found three shelters for homeless children in New Orleans. They were in different parts of the city. She located the one closest to the bus station on the map. It was only half a mile east, halfway to the river. Rowan could walk the distance.

The shelter was called the Miriam Winslet Shelter for Homeless and Trafficked Children.

3

DAY ONE - FRENCH QUARTER, 2100 HRS

"Cops have a lot more important things to do than look for a thirteen-year-old kid," Ellie says. "We just needed to let the fuss blow over."

The weather has turned foul and cold. Stinging rain lashes the windows of the Jean Lafitte. The blurred figures of tourists run past us on Royal, splashing through puddles. Several hotel guests dash through the alley and into the courtyard, desperate to get to their rooms.

I'm glad we decided to talk in the hotel restaurant.

"That's true," I say, "but how did you know the shelter would accept her?"

"I didn't, but there were two others we could try. In the end, we got lucky. It's not hard to get into a shelter, if you know what you're doing. I have practice, remember?"

"I know you do. But it can't have been easy to coach Rowan."

"I told her to tell them the truth. That Dad abused her and she ran away. The important thing was to give them a phony name and refuse to tell them where Mom and Dad live. It's totally credible—she's afraid to be sent back. The staff are used to kids who lie, and the staff want to help."

Ellie takes a sip of her beer and continues, "Some places demand a referee. A case worker, a police officer, a therapist. Anything. You only have referees if you have been in the system for a while. Not everyone can provide a referee, so there are always places willing to take in children who don't. I looked up the name of a doctor in Perdido, gave Rowan a burner number in case she was forced to provide a contact. If they called, I would answer. Of course, they would follow up. Ask for more information. There would be all the usual discussions about what's best for the child. But I only needed Rowan to lie low for a few days. After that, I'd have her on a bus to Pensacola."

"What went wrong?"

"Rowan was accepted into the Miriam Winslet Shelter. It's a grand old mansion in the Garden District. Some wealthy widow bequeathed it to a charity for abused children. Rowan stayed there for two days."

"Did the staff call the burner?"

"No. They listened to Rowan's story and didn't ask for a reference."

"Isn't that unusual?"

"Not in this case. She told them the truth—mostly. She didn't want to tell them who or where her parents were. So asking her for a reference was pointless."

"So everything went according to plan."

"Until she stopped replying to messages."

Ellie followed Rowan to New Orleans.

ELLIE LEANED back in the front passenger seat of Miriam Winslet's four-door Taurus sedan. Inexpensive, clean and well maintained, it was the perfect vehicle for a frugal charity. The caseworker driving the car was a nicely turned-out young man in his late twenties. The kind of guy who graduated Tulane with a degree in sociology. Buttoned-down Oxford shirt and a crew-neck cotton sweater. His name was Oliver.

"Wow." Ellie looked about herself in wonder. "These are mansions."

They were driving along St. Charles Avenue, next to the streetcar line. The streetcar, operated since 1853, was the oldest running streetcar in the world. On either side was the Garden District. Built on an old plantation, plots of green nestled among ancient oak trees, huge houses of Italianate and Gothic revival style.

"The biggest is seventy thousand square feet," Oliver said. "Our place isn't nearly as grand."

Oliver stopped at a light, waited for green, and turned left down a narrow, leafy street. Apart from the huge houses, it felt like an unpretentious, upper-middle-class suburb. Late-model cars and SUVs were parked on both sides of the street, with room to drive in between.

"Here we are." Oliver gestured toward a large, two-story Italianate house with fine cast-iron galleries. Like every place else in the district, the gardens were populated with venerable oaks and lush plantings. The house was surrounded by a high wrought-iron fence and swinging gates. The fence posts were fashioned into black iron spikes entwined with climbing green vines and yellow flowers.

Oliver pulled the sedan into a concrete driveway. A detached carriage house stood some twenty yards from the

Miriam Winslet House. Two stories, the ground floor was used as a garage. There was a door on the left and a large garage door on the right. Ellie guessed the door on the left opened onto a flight of stairs that led to the second-floor living quarters.

The carriage house was set two car lengths back from the gate. The door opened, and a man stepped out and unlocked the gate with an electronic fob. He swung the gate open and waved Oliver through.

"Thanks, Des."

Des was forty years old, six feet tall, and powerfully built. "Des is our driver and groundskeeper," Oliver said. "He occupies the carriage house."

"Do you live here?"

"Not a chance. I'm just the professional help."

Oliver parked the sedan behind a shiny black Jeep Cherokee. Got out of the car and led Ellie up a paved walk toward the main house. Ellie stared at the cornice that topped the structure. The house was two stories, but the interior must have been high-ceilinged. There was such distance between the second story and the cornice that there was plenty of room for an attic floor. Ellie could see a pair of chimneys jutting from the roof. Beneath them, the attic windows looked like eyes. The second-floor rooms had French windows that opened onto a balcony with wrought-iron rails. All were decorated with hanging baskets of flowers and ferns.

There were steps leading to a porch that surrounded the ground floor. Oliver led Ellie to the front door. Wicker furniture was arranged on the porch. A girl of about eighteen was sitting in a deep lounge chair, reading a book. The girl looked up as they approached.

"Kate, this is Ellie," Oliver said. "Ellie will be staying with us for a while."

The girls greeted each other.

Kate acted as though Ellie's arrival was nothing new. Oliver opened the front door and led Ellie into the foyer.

She'd been right about the ceilings. They were at least eighteen feet high. To the left was a large sitting room with comfortable furniture, a widescreen television, and bookshelves. Several children were watching TV.

To the right was a dining room with a grand dining table and places for twenty guests. Immediately ahead was a wide corridor stretching to the back of the ground floor. A spiral mahogany staircase led to the second floor.

They were greeted by a tall, middle-aged woman. Ellie thought she must be fifty, but she was attractive and looked young. She had shoulder-length chestnut hair and a practiced smile. There was something about the woman that Ellie found unusual. She realized that the woman's clothing belonged to another era. Conservative clothing was meant to stand the test of time. Such styles didn't change much, but designs changed in subtle ways, and materials could vary. The woman's blouse, skirt and jacket seemed to be from the 1940s. When she looked a second time, Ellie realized the woman's hair was made up in a style more suited to the Second World War.

"You must be Ellie." The woman reached forward and took Ellie's hand. Her grip was dry and firm. "I'm Victoria Calthorpe. Call me Victoria. I'm the superintendent of Miriam Winslet."

"Pleased to meet you."

Victoria released Ellie's hand and turned to Oliver. "Have you checked her bag?"

Apologetic but thorough, Oliver had checked Ellie's haversack for contraband. Drugs or weapons. "Yes, ma'am. It's alright."

"There's a set of rules posted in your room," Victoria told Ellie. "Any violations can lead to expulsion from the home. Tomorrow, Oliver will take you to the hospital for a standard checkup."

"Checkup?"

"All our children have regular checkups. The majority have been abused or trafficked. They need to be checked for pregnancy, STDs, drug use. You understand."

"Of course."

Victoria shrugged. "An unpleasant process, but necessary. We can take it from here, Oliver."

The young man nodded. "Good luck," he said to Ellie. Then he turned and left.

"We'll take things slowly and let you get used to the place," Victoria said. "You'll meet Ollie once a week to start, then twice. There's no set schedule. The idea is to get to know each other and find ways to help you."

Ellie said nothing. Her eyes were searching her surroundings, looking for any sign of Rowan.

Victoria took a small radio from a black leather holster on her belt and keyed the transmit button. "Jasmine, please come to the foyer."

A black woman of about forty joined them. She was dressed in a peach-colored dress and flat-heeled shoes. At her waist was a thin belt with a holster for her own radio. Oliver hadn't worn one. Maybe he left his in the car. Ellie couldn't remember if Des was similarly equipped. She guessed he was.

Staff at other shelters relied on telephones. The Miriam

Winslet Shelter was beginning to look more like a secure facility.

"Yes, ma'am," the black woman said.

"Jasmine, this is Ellie. She'll be joining us." Victoria turned back to Ellie. "Jasmine and her husband, Richard, cook and keep the house. You'll get to know them well. Jasmine, please show Ellie to her room. Ellie, you're free until six o'clock. At that time, we gather for dinner. If you need me, I'll be in my office. It's at the back of the ground floor."

Ellie watched Victoria turn on her heel and walk away. Jasmine smiled. "Come with me," she said. "I'll show you around."

Jasmine led the way up the spiral staircase. As they climbed, Ellie ran the flat of her hand over the polished banister. "We have seven children with us now," Jasmine said, "yourself included. There are ten rooms on the second floor, and four more in the attic. We use some rooms for storage space but can free them up if need be."

"Are you ever full?" Ellie asked.

"Oh, yes. But the numbers change a great deal. We're selective about who we accept."

Ellie found that strange. She'd applied at a number of shelters in the past and found Miriam Winslet easy to get into. Maybe it was because they weren't full and needed to keep their numbers up to retain funding.

A black man Jasmine's age emerged from a chamber at the top of the stairs. His hair was graying at the temples. He wore a white dress shirt, polished black shoes, dark trousers, and black suspenders. Sure enough, he had a radio holstered at his hip. "The room's ready."

"Thanks, Richard. This is Ellie."

"Nice to meet you, miss," Richard said.

Jasmine stepped to the door of the chamber. Its door was of heavy, aged wood. A black plastic pad was set against the wall next to the doorknob. The kind you slap a card against to unlock the door. Jasmine turned the knob without tapping a card against the pad. The door wasn't locked. She ushered Ellie into the chamber.

Ellie found herself in a beautiful room with a king-sized four-poster bed, a thick comforter, and stuffed pillows. The bed was built in eighteenth-century French style, with intricately carved columns and headboard. There was a dresser and stool and a big closet. The closet was empty, and Ellie was conscious she did not have any clothes except for a change of T-shirt and underwear in her haversack.

"There are places in town where you can buy inexpensive clothing," Jasmine said. "Richard can take you tomorrow."

The housekeeper went to the French windows and threw the center frames open. A fresh breeze carried the scent of magnolias into the room. Ellie could see the blue sky, the carriage house below, and the roofs of neighboring mansions among the high oak trees. She stepped onto the balcony and put her hands on the black wrought-iron rail. Drew in a breath.

"Nothing like fresh air to make a body feel alive," Jasmine said. "I'll leave you now. Come down to dinner at six. Be sure to close the windows. Weather's awful uncertain, and when it rains, it pours."

"Thank you, Jasmine."

The housekeeper left and closed the door behind her. Ellie stepped to the bed and threw herself backwards onto the comforter. Clasped her hands behind her head and stared at the ceiling.

No sign of Rowan. Ellie had given her sister six hours to charge her phone in case it had died on her. When Rowan still didn't answer, Ellie packed some things and took a bus to New Orleans. She'd found a hotel on Chartres Street, not far from Jackson Square. Made herself comfortable, and planned her approach to the Miriam Winslet Shelter. The next day, she'd walked into the charity's office in the Warehouse District. She put on her nervous runaway act and said hello to Oliver.

There she was, in the lair of the beast. The question was, where was Rowan?

The easy part was over.

THE BEDROOM DOOR didn't lock automatically. Ellie hadn't been given a pass card, and there was no way to lock the door from the inside. Guests at the Miriam Winslet Shelter were not permitted privacy. There was a laminated 8½" by 11" sheet of rules taped to the inside of the door.

Ellie stepped into the hall, closed the door behind her, then turned the knob and pushed it open. No question, it wouldn't lock without the pass card. And the pass card worked differently than hotel pass cards. In hotels, the doors locked automatically and the pass card opened them. It didn't work that way at Miriam Winslet House.

She went downstairs, carrying her haversack. She'd already decided not to leave anything in her room. She walked down the hall toward the back of the ground floor. There were several chambers on the left with closed doors.

The corner chamber had a gold plaque with black lettering that read *Victoria Calthorpe*.

A woman's voice issued from behind the door. Victoria was on the phone. Ellie held her breath and listened.

"The new girl arrived this afternoon… She's going to the hospital tomorrow for her checkup… Yes, you can meet her then, if you want."

Silence. Victoria must have put the phone down.

Ellie glanced around. At the end of the hall was a back door that probably led to a yard. To the right, an open door and a large, airy sitting room. French doors opened to a back porch. Ubiquitous brightly colored flowers hung in baskets among wicker deck furniture.

Next to the back sitting room was a large, modern kitchen. Jasmine and Richard were puttering around, preparing dinner. Ellie went out the back door and walked around the house. Made her way to the front, where she joined Kate.

"It's nice out here," Ellie said.

Kate looked up from her book. "It's a gilded cage."

"What do you mean?"

"You stay because it's nice, and there's nowhere else to go." Kate looked toward the carriage house, where Des was washing the Jeep Cherokee. "How do you like the lock on your bedroom door?"

"It *is* unusual."

"You can't lock it without a card. Only the staff have cards. So they can lock us in and let us out if they want."

"Have you been locked in?"

"No, and I've never seen them lock anyone in. But they can do it." Kate closed her book, marking her place with a finger. She leaned back in the wicker chair. "I'm leaving tomorrow."

"Why?"

"This place gives me the creeps. The girl who came before you thought so too. Stayed all of two days."

Ellie's heart jumped. "Who was she? Where did she go?"

"Rowan something or other. One morning she never came down to breakfast. Victoria had Des and Richard out looking for her."

"Did they call the police?"

"Yes. The NOPD came over, looked through her room, didn't find anything. But they were worried, especially after Bailey ran off and was found murdered. It made the papers. Police came by and spent an hour with Victoria."

"Wait a minute." Ellie's heart was pounding in her chest. "What do you mean, murdered?"

"I mean *dead*. Happened a couple of months ago. He went missing, turned up in the swamp. Up toward Baton Rouge."

"Do you think this other girl…"

Kate shrugged. "There's no reason to think like that. But the place still gives me the creeps, so I'm out of here."

THE MORNING SUNSHINE had given way to a deep overcast by dinner. New Orleans was lush and green for a reason—it rained a lot. Ellie had closed the French windows against the wind, which had grown steadily colder, and the heavy clouds with bellies of lead.

After dinner, Ellie went up to her room, turned out the lights, and lay in bed. She had every reason to fear for

Rowan's safety. If Rowan had left the home willingly, she would have her phone, and she would be reachable. No, something had happened to her.

Ellie became conscious of the wind. It whistled through the leaves and branches of the oaks. Rattled the windows of the great house. She wanted to crawl under the comforter, but she didn't want to fall asleep. The cold kept her alert.

How could she find out what happened to Rowan? She wanted to look at Rowan's room, but she didn't know which one it was. She'd have to find a way to ask someone. Slip the question casually into conversation. There would be opportunities.

But there were other ways to find things out. Victoria Calthorpe would have files on Miriam Winslet's guests. At a minimum, their application forms. The results of their health checkups, therapy notes, progress with their schoolwork. Those records might be kept on paper or online. Possibly both.

Ellie had to get into Victoria Calthorpe's office.

Well past midnight, Ellie rolled out of bed and pushed open her door. It swung aside on well-oiled hinges. Apparently, Richard was diligent in his work. The hall was dark save for dim tungsten bulbs at either end and along the spiral staircase that led to the ground floor. A straight staircase, also dimly lit, led to the attic.

Ellie stood still and listened. She could hear the wind rattling the windows on the ground floor where the sitting rooms were open to the main hall. On the second floor, it moaned around the house like a living thing, and the walls creaked like old bones. There were no *human* sounds she could detect.

The mahogany banister provided support as Ellie

descended the staircase. She was careful not to trip. When she got to the bottom, she studied the hall. There was a dim light over the back door, another over the front. The hall was dark. She walked slowly toward the back.

When she got to the end, she looked into the back sitting room. Light from a single streetlamp filtered into the space, and the furniture threw long shadows into the hall.

Ellie turned to Victoria Calthorpe's office and tried the doorknob. The door was locked. It had a black plastic pad to the right of the knob. Only staff had pass cards, and Ellie guessed only Victoria Calthorpe could edit the permissions coded into the cards. There was no getting past *that* lock.

The French windows weren't sturdy. She could break into her own room from the balcony. Maybe she could break into Victoria's office from the porch. She went to the back door and tried the knob.

Her heart jumped in her chest. The doorknob wouldn't budge. There was a black plastic pad next to this one too. Kate was right. The locks made sense in a creepy sort of way. Anyone with a pass card could get out of the house at night. The guests, without pass cards, were prisoners.

The front door was also locked, as Ellie knew it would be. Like an animal that had just tested the boundaries of its cage, Ellie went back upstairs. She took off her running shoes and jeans. Crawled into bed and pulled the comforter up to her chin.

Try as she might, Ellie couldn't sleep. A young boy from the Miriam Winslet Shelter was dead, and Rowan was missing.

4

DAY ONE - FRENCH QUARTER, 2300 HRS

Midday, mixed sun and cloud. Lost in thought, Ellie sat in the front passenger seat of the Miriam Winslet sedan. She stared out the window at the endless blue-gray expanse of Lake Pontchartrain.

"Penny for your thoughts." Oliver guided the car away from the international airport in Kenner and turned onto an exit ramp marked Resurrection.

Ellie wouldn't share her thoughts for a dollar. "Why is the hospital all the way out here?"

"Our guests don't have insurance. Miriam Winslet provides care through a partnership with Resurrection General. It's a private hospital that serves Resurrection Parish and parts of neighboring parishes like Orleans, Jefferson and Saint John. They provide their services to the charity free of charge."

In the distance, Ellie saw the blue-gray of Lake Pontchartrain turn to green swampland. Forests of bald cypress trees stood with their roots and lower trunks submerged in the salty waters of the lake. Here and there grew scattered patches of swamp tupelo. A long highway bore traffic to the north shore of the lake. Ellie realized that most of what she was looking at was swamp.

"That's Lake Pontchartrain to the right," Oliver said. "It's a tidal estuary, connected to the Gulf of Mexico by the Rigolets. To the left is Lake Maurepas. This, here, is Resurrection. Not very big, but it's the parish seat. The parish is shaped like a slice of pie. The wide end is along the swamp, and the point sticks right into Jefferson and Saint John. The town of Resurrection is in the middle."

Ellie wondered if she should ask about the dead boy, Bailey. Decided it wouldn't do to arouse suspicion before she had a chance to carry out her plan.

Resurrection wasn't very big, but it seemed like everything one might expect from small-town America. They drove down the main street. There was a town hall, post office, gas station, and roadside diner. On the other side of town, a large road sign announced that they were approaching Resurrection General Hospital.

"The hospital is on the south side of town." Oliver was used to playing tour guide. Ellie got the feeling it was his job to take new Miriam Winslet guests for their checkups. A canned tour was a good way to keep them calm. "It's central to Jefferson and the other parishes."

Ellie could see the hospital a quarter of a mile down a side road. It was a modern three-story affair. Not very big, but one didn't expect a big hospital here. Resurrection General was a private facility, and that meant a profit-motivated business. Its site had been carefully chosen with an eye to real estate value, construction costs, and the size of the market it would serve.

There weren't many cars in the parking lot. Oliver parked the sedan, and they got out and walked inside. Ellie's senses were immediately assailed by the sights and smells shared by all hospitals. The pervasive smell of disinfectant. The aroma of cheap hospital food. Elderly people in wheelchairs, patients in hospital gowns walking around while dragging their IVs on wheeled poles. Orderlies pushed other patients around on gurneys.

Oliver went to the reception desk and spoke with a clerk. A nurse came out to greet them.

"Ellie, this is Karen Shelly."

"Nice to meet you, Ellie."

The woman's hand was soft and warm. A middle-aged woman, charming and approachable. Not at all like stern Victoria Calthorpe. Ellie returned Nurse Shelly's gentle pressure and released her hand.

"You'll be here several hours," Nurse Shelly told her. "For the first hour, we'll take information from you. Miriam Winslet has already given us your basics. We'll be asking you things like if you've had measles, that sort of thing. We'll take samples for tests. Some blood, a few swabs. I'll do most of that myself. When that's done, the doctor will come in and give you a thorough physical."

"When can we start?" Ellie asked. The sooner they started, the sooner she could get out of there. She hated the smell of disinfectant in hospitals. Hated passing rooms where patients moaned with pain.

"I'll be back in a couple of hours." Oliver went to the car.

Nurse Shelly took her to a small examination room. Fired up a tablet, logged in, and started filling in forms. "We've done away with patient charts," she said. "It's all digital nowadays. We have one of these in every room, more at the nurses' stations."

Ellie had to answer an endless stream of questions. Her vaccination history. Onset of first period. How regular her periods were. All the childhood diseases she could remember having. Had she ever had an STD? Had she ever been diagnosed with cytomegalovirus? Hepatitis B? Hepatitis C? HIV? Nurse Shelly went through every single infection that might have been transmitted by sex or intravenous drug use. Had she ever had surgery? Was she aware of issues with blood clotting?

Some of the questions seemed needlessly invasive. It didn't matter. Ellie was an accomplished liar. But then, they were sure to cross-check her responses against other tests.

When the battery of questions was complete, Nurse Shelly took bloods. Ellie thought that procedure was normally done by a phlebotomist. Nurse Shelly maintained strict control of the process. She was uncompromisingly thorough. When the bloods were done, she had Ellie strip and put on a hospital gown. Measured her height and weight, then made her sit on the edge of an examination table.

"Some of this may seem alarming," Nurse Shelly said. "Please understand, it's all routine, and I'll finish as quickly as possible. Everyone has to go through it, okay?"

"Okay." Ellie parked her apprehension. She understood why Nurse Shelly handled everything. Her bedside manner was faultless. The nurse drew on a pair of latex gloves and lined up a row of plastic vials and swabs.

The nurse took several buccal swabs.

"Why so many?" Ellie asked.

"Because we test for different things."

Nurse Shelly had Ellie lie down for a vaginal swab. Then she said, "Roll onto your side and pull up your knees."

Nurse Shelly couldn't be serious. Ellie hesitated.

"It'll just take a second," the nurse said.

Ellie did as she was told. Nurse Shelly patted her shoulder reassuringly. There was a brief penetration, a twist, and a withdrawal. The nurse stepped away and capped the plastic sample vial with an air of finality. "There," she said. "All done. You can get up now."

As if on cue, there was a knock on the door. A man in a white lab coat stepped into the room. Fifty years old, with dark curly hair, a narrow face, and wire-framed glasses.

"Ellie, this is Dr. Emile Durand."

"Hi," Ellie said.

"It's nice to meet you, Ellie." Dr. Durand barely looked up from his tablet. He was reviewing the notes Nurse Shelly had taken. He clucked and hummed. "Alright, let us begin."

Nurse Shelly excused herself. Ellie had felt comfortable with the nurse, but Dr. Durand treated her like a lab rat. What was it about phones and electronic devices that kept people glued to them? Didn't people look at each other anymore?

The tests Dr. Durand conducted surprised Ellie. It wasn't that they were bizarre, or Ellie had never seen them done on TV before. They were the kinds of tests she would never have expected to be part of a routine physical.

Dr. Durand made her lie back and open her gown. Then he took an electrocardiogram. Apprehensively, Ellie watched the machine plot the activity of her heart. The tracings were automatically saved to a digital file. Then the doctor performed an echocardiogram. Made her lie back in different positions while he moved a sensor over the front and sides of her chest.

By the time he was finished, it was late afternoon.

"Thank you, Ellie." Durand got up and made more notes in his tablet. "You can get dressed now."

The doctor didn't leave the room while she dressed, but she didn't feel uncomfortable. Durand barely glanced at her. Ellie felt a faint stab of outrage. Damn, she was a pretty girl. Men undressed her with their eyes all the time. Here, this doctor had her naked in an exam room and couldn't care less.

Durand took a phone from his pocket and hit a speed dial. "Karen? I'm finished here."

Ellie sat in a chair and laced up her running shoes. "May I go?"

"Wait here," Durand said. "Everything seems in order; Nurse Shelly will finish up your paperwork and release you to Miriam Winslet. If anything of note shows up in the tests, we'll be in touch."

With that, the doctor left Ellie staring at the wall.

NURSE SHELLY GUIDED Ellie back to the reception area. There, Dr. Durand was speaking with a man wearing an expensive, charcoal-colored suit. The man was in his fifties, built like a football quarterback. He had wavy black hair, a broad face, and full, sensual lips. His complexion was swarthy, like he was Arabic or Italian.

The man spotted them walking down the corridor. He turned and greeted them. "Karen."

"Hello, Mark."

"Is this Miriam Winslet's new guest?"

"Yes. This is Ellie. Ellie, this is Mark Luka. He owns Resurrection General."

"Very nice to meet you." Ellie shook Luka's hand. He had a firm grip, but was careful to apply light pressure.

"Ellie, if you have any health concerns, anything at all, we're here for you. Resurrection General takes great pleasure in giving back to the community."

Nurse Shelly touched Ellie's elbow and guided her to the entrance, where Oliver was waiting. Ellie couldn't shake a feeling of deep unease. Nurse Shelly had been nice to her. The doctor had been one hundred percent professional.

But Ellie felt violated.

It was dusk before Oliver and Ellie got back to Miriam Winslet. Once again, the sky had gone overcast, and Ellie wondered if it would rain. As Oliver pulled into the driveway, she studied the structure of the main house.

Des pulled the passenger door open for her, and Ellie got out.

"See you tomorrow," Oliver said.

Ellie waved goodbye, and Oliver backed onto the street. Des closed the gates behind him. Backed the Jeep up to the gate, opened the garage door, and backed a Chevy minivan up to the Jeep. Des closed the garage door, uncoiled the garden hose, and began washing down the Chevy.

Des was wearing a radio in a holster at his hip.

Ellie squinted at the sky. It would be dark in half an hour. She walked toward the house. If she hurried, she would be in time for dinner. But she had no appetite.

The more she studied the house, the more convinced Ellie became that her plan would work. Her room was in the middle of the second floor, two doors down from Victoria Calthorpe's. She was free to step out onto her balcony at any time, and it was no trouble to roll over the rail and make her way onto one of the thin metal pillars that supported the balcony and connected it to the porch below.

It wouldn't be hard for Ellie to slide or shimmy down the pillar. The Italianate design was ornate, with a Roman Doric shaft, fluted at the base, with narrow circular shelves. The shelves would provide finger and toeholds on her way back up. She'd go down in running shoes. Climbing back, she'd tie her shoes together by the laces, drape them over her shoulders, and go up barefoot. She had become adept at climbing obstacles in the New York underground.

Ellie just needed to wait for the right time.

5

DAY TWO - FRENCH QUARTER, 0000 HRS

"This place gives me the creeps," Kate had said. Ellie knew exactly what she meant. The thought of Rowan enduring the physical examination she had gone through made her angry.

After dinner, Ellie went to the living room and watched television with the others. There was an argument over what to watch, a squabble over DVDs. Ellie closed her eyes and switched off until the others settled on some brainless comedy. Then she built a mental picture of the outside of the house and rehearsed her movements.

One by one, children went to their rooms. At eleven o'clock, Victoria called lights out, and the stragglers went to bed. Ellie lay on her comforter, fully clothed, staring at the dark. At three in the morning, she swung her legs off the bed, slung her haversack over her shoulder and across her chest, and went to the French doors that opened to her balcony. She swung them wide and stepped into the night.

The night was pleasantly cool. It was windy, but not as bad as the previous night. The oak leaves rustled, and the branches swayed. Ellie smelled the fragrance of the trees, scented with the gauzy ferns and tropical flowers that hung in the baskets. The baskets traced short arcs in the breeze, their shadows making complex patterns on the wall.

Ellie took a breath and swung herself up onto the balcony rail. Looked down and made her way to a spot directly over one of the pillars. Then she lowered herself carefully. Held on to the rail, leaned back into space, and braced the soles of her runners against the floor of the balcony.

Moving slowly was asking for trouble, as was moving too quickly. Ellie executed the movements she had rehearsed a hundred times in her mind. Lowered herself until she could grip the pillar with both hands. The texture of the black-painted iron was exactly as she had imagined it. She felt with the toes of her running shoes for the narrow shelves on the Doric shaft, each scarcely an inch deep.

Three minutes later, Ellie was standing on the porch rail. She swung herself around the rail like a pole dancer and dropped, catlike, to the porch.

She walked to the end of the building, stopped outside Victoria's office. Her eyes had adjusted to the dim light. Ellie had excellent night vision, developed from two years in the tunnels under New York. She examined the French doors. As she expected, they were like those on her own room.

A plastic rewards card was all it took to slip the lock. Ellie swung the doors open, stepped inside, and closed them behind her.

Victoria furnished her office as conservatively as she furnished herself. The mahogany furniture was heavy and dated to the early twentieth century. There was a big kneehole desk and a laptop open on a leather scuff protector. Multicolored planets orbited each other on the screensaver.

A leather recliner for Victoria. Two wing chairs, bookshelves, and... a filing cabinet.

With the curtains open, there was enough light filtering from outside for her to see, but not enough to work. Ellie needed more light. She drew the curtains shut and turned on her phone's flashlight.

Ellie went straight to the filing cabinet. Swore under her breath. Rowan had given Miriam Winslet her correct first name and a phony last name. Less to remember, and it sounded authentic. But Ellie didn't know what last name Rowan had given. That meant she had to go through all the files from A to Z looking for Rowan. She couldn't think of an easy way to narrow down her search.

She slid open the first file drawer. Sure enough, it contained files on Miriam Winslet's guests. There were four drawers in vertical order. Ellie looked for her own file. It was exactly where she expected to find it. The folder contained only one sheet of paper—her application.

But it confirmed that she was on the right track. She put her file folder back. Returned to the top drawer and began going through the files one by one, looking for Rowan. It didn't take long. Her sister was at the end of the second file drawer. Rowan Miller. How creative.

Rowan's file was a quarter of an inch thick. There was her application. The rest of the file consisted entirely of her medical checkup. Ellie didn't understand most of it. There were Rowan's answers to the same questions Nurse Shelly had asked Ellie that afternoon. Results of the tests.

Ellie laid the file flat on the desk and photographed every page. When she was done, she replaced the file in the cabinet and slid the drawer shut. She could examine the contents at her leisure.

Victoria's recliner was comfortable. Ellie settled into it and pressed the escape key to bring up the login screen. It asked for a password. Ellie pressed enter. Wrong. She tried *password* in lowercase. Wrong. *PASSWORD* in uppercase. Wrong.

That kind of guessing wasn't going to get Ellie anywhere. She opened the top-left drawer and looked inside. Nothing likely. She felt with her fingertips along the bottom of the drawer hole, then the bottom of the drawer itself.

Taped there was a small piece of paper. Ellie picked at the edge of the tape with her fingernail. Pried it up, then peeled it off. The paper was a yellow sticky with a word written on it. *V@ctWinsleto!*

An icy breeze raised the hairs on the back of Ellie's neck. She turned to look at the French doors. A gust of wind rattled the glass panes, squeezed past moldings warped with age, billowed the curtains she had drawn to conceal her flashlight. The damn creepy house was getting to her.

Ellie hammered the password into the machine and hit enter.

The login screen dissolved and revealed Victoria Calthorpe's desktop. The wallpaper was generic. A dozen shortcuts were arranged along the bottom of the screen. There was a shortcut to the browser, a folder labeled *VC*, a folder labeled *Guests,* and a folder labeled *Videos.*

Ellie took the yellow sticky, taped it back in place, and slid the drawer shut. Then she turned back to the laptop and clicked on *Guests*. She quickly realized it contained softcopies of all the files in the filing cabinet. She found Rowan's, zipped it, and emailed it to herself. Then she went into the sent items folder and deleted the message.

This was too easy.

Bailey was next. Like Rowan, she didn't know his last name. But it was easy to go down the list of folders in detail view until she found one with the first name Bailey. She checked to make sure there was only one, then zipped and mailed that too. Deleted the sent message. Checked her phone to make sure she'd received the emails.

She could spend all night doing this.

Ellie clicked on the *Videos* folder.

There were a number of subfolders. *Interviews, Therapy Sessions, Security*.

Ellie went into the *Security* folder. Lit the keyboard with her flashlight and pressed the *Mute* key. She didn't want to find that the volume was cranked up to the max when she hit play.

There were dozens of files. They were named according to a convention. *Front_Fence_DDMMYYYY. Back_Fence_DDMMYYYY* and so on.

Ellie's stomach hollowed.

Miriam Winslet was fitted with hidden cameras. They weren't monitored twenty-four seven, but they recorded continuously and could be reviewed.

Front_Sitting_Room_DDMMYYYY

Back_Sitting_Room_DDMMYYYY

Bedroom01_DDMMYYYY

Shit.

Victoria had the whole house covered. Had Ellie's bedroom covered. She was cooked.

Ellie was ready to lock the laptop and leave when she noticed a filename that stood out.

Rowan_Main_Hall

What was *that* all about? Ellie double-clicked the file.

A video player opened up on the screen, and a night-vision image flickered to life. It was black and blue-white phosphor, high-quality commercial light amplification. Breed had shown Ellie military-grade night vision. This imagery wasn't as good, but it was good enough.

The camera was positioned in the center of the hall, looking toward the foyer and front door. A young girl stepped carefully down the spiral staircase and approached the door. She was slender and wore jeans and a light jacket. Her long, straight hair fell past her shoulders.

Rowan.

She went to the front door and tried to open it. The door was locked. She hesitated. Anxiety stamped on her features, she turned to face the camera. Hurried toward the lens. She was going to try the back door.

The camera perspective reversed 180 degrees. Ellie realized the recording had switched to another camera, facing the other way. Camera perspective was automatically guided by motion sensors. Rowan hurried to the back door, found it also locked.

A male figure stepped into the frame. Ellie recognized Des by his posture and build. He advanced on Rowan. She must have heard him, for she turned and dodged past. It was hard to do that in the narrow hall, but Rowan was quick. Des lunged for her, but she dove for the floor, too low for him to reach. She scrambled on her belly, got to her feet and ran... right into Victoria.

It was impossible to mistake Victoria's tall, broad-shouldered frame. She grabbed Rowan by the arms. The young girl struggled, but she was caught in a vise. Des took Rowan's left arm from Victoria and twisted it up behind her shoulder blades. The pain on Rowan's face was unmistakable. She started to scream, but Des clamped his other hand over her mouth.

Ellie's fists clenched.

The video ended. Ellie closed the video player, emailed the video to herself, and deleted the email from the sent items folder. Heart pounding, she logged out of the laptop and turned off her flashlight. Sat in the dark and waited to calm down.

A floorboard creaked in the hall.

Ellie got to her feet and pushed the recliner back.

The office door opened. Richard stepped into the room and flicked the light switch. The glare blinded Ellie.

"Now you stay right there, young lady."

There was nothing polite or deferential in Richard's tone. He stepped around the desk and reached for Ellie. She clutched her phone in her right fist and slammed the bottom edge of the phone against the bridge of his nose. Richard's nose broke and blood spurted over his mouth. As he raised his hands to his face, she hit him again, cracking the edge of the phone against his right temple. Opened up a cut over his eye.

Richard staggered sideways against the desk and went down. Ellie turned, flung open the French doors and ran to the porch rail. Looked back, saw Richard clawing his radio from the holster on his hip. She jumped the rail and sprinted for the front gate.

The gate would be locked. She had to get over it.

Ellie passed the Chevy minivan just as the carriage house door swung open and Des launched himself at her. She jumped for the Jeep Cherokee and scrambled onto its hood. Turned as Des tried to grab her. Dodged, aimed a kick at his face, hit him in the mouth.

Running on pure adrenaline, Ellie bounded from the hood and onto the Jeep's roof. The vehicle was backed against the gate and she could jump for it. Her hands closed on the top rail, between the posts. She reached up with her right leg. Careful not to catch herself on the ornamental spears, she swung over the top.

A heartbeat's hesitation and Ellie jumped to the ground. Turned and ran north toward St. Charles Avenue.

There was a roar behind her. She'd made it two hundred yards down the dark street when the Jeep Cherokee reversed at speed. Des backed into the street and snapped the vehicle into a turn so sharp it rocked on its suspension. He threw it into drive and raced after Ellie.

Ellie couldn't outrun a Jeep. She dodged down a side street, then jinked left between houses. Des tore around the block to try to head her off. She skidded to a stop, jinked right and ran between another pair of houses. Des raced by, realized he'd overshot, and screeched to a halt. She kept running.

All these snazzy SUVs weren't really made for off-road use. Not without heavy modification. Big tires, elevated chassis. They were showpieces parents use to take their kids to the PTA. Ellie had to get off the paved roads.

Ellie ran between houses, between trees. She wished there were more cars on the street. It would have made it harder for Des to follow her. Four o'clock in the morning, and the streets were empty. Already, Des was throwing caution to the wind, tearing up pristine lawns and crushing carefully manicured hedges.

She found herself running across an open road. A

complex of buildings reared up against the night sky. A sign read:

LOUISE S. MCGEHEE SCHOOL

It looked like a school. A collection of large buildings arranged into a campus and joined by connecting structures. All were two or three stories tall. The complex was surrounded by trees and a low, black-painted iron fence. The grounds were lit by streetlamps around the perimeter and floodlamps on the rooftops.

Ellie was running toward a beautiful Renaissance-style building on the western edge of the complex. Scaffolding had been erected against the west side, and it looked like the structure was in the process of maintenance or renovation. The fence had been carefully taken down to allow construction vehicles access to the grounds. Lumber, bricks, sacks of cement and other construction materials were piled on the lawn.

Ellie sprinted for the school. If she could get between the buildings, if she could get into the school itself, Des wouldn't be able to follow her with the Jeep. He'd have to dismount. She ran through the gaping hole in the fence line, straight for the building that was under renovation.

She reached the field of construction materials. The Jeep was almost on top of her. Ellie dodged behind the pile of lumber, and Des snapped the wheel right to avoid a collision. She ran toward the brick pile, and he gunned the engine. She looked back. His face was a mask, garishly lit by the floodlights.

Ellie stumbled and sprawled in the dirt. The Jeep continued past, screeched to a stop and swung around. Turf and clods of dirt scattered in a fan ten feet high. Des pointed the machine at her and floored the gas. The LED headlights were blinding. Ellie grabbed a brick. Hard, rough and gritty against her fingers. Heavy in her hand. She rose to one knee and hurled it with all her strength. Felt the muscles of her arm and shoulder stretch like elastic bands. Watched the brick sail over the Jeep's hood. She dove behind the sacks of cement.

The brick smashed the Jeep's window right in front of the driver's face. Des lost control and the Jeep crashed into the sacks with a loud thump.

Ellie coughed from the cloud of cement dust thrown onto her from the sacks. Staggered to her feet. The Jeep's engine had died, and Des was struggling to get it going. She ran between the buildings. A big three-story structure to her right and a two-story wing to her left. Flattened herself against a wall and looked back.

Des had the engine running and was backing toward the street. There were shouts from the other side of the school. Security guards ran around the corner. Des drove out of sight. The guards looked around the construction site. They'd arrived late and didn't see Ellie hide in the shadows.

Ellie lost herself in the school grounds and emerged on the other side of the campus. Made her way to St. Charles Avenue and jumped the fence. She didn't want to walk on St. Charles, where she could be seen. Instead, she headed east on a side road a block south.

Limping, Ellie only wanted to get back to her hotel in the French Quarter. She and Rowan were in deep trouble, and she needed help.

She needed Breed.

I sit across from Ellie in the hotel coffee shop. I've finished watching the video of Rowan's struggle with Des and Victoria Calthorpe. The big man twisting the little girl's arm behind her back. If only he'd try that on me. I push the thought from my mind. Remind myself none of this is personal. I stare at Ellie.

"You said those men must have followed you from your hotel."

"I went straight from my hotel to the Ruby Slipper," Ellie says. "I don't know how else they could have known I would be there."

"What name did you use to check into your hotel?"

"Not Mary Louise Kennan."

"One of your other identities."

"Yes."

"Whoever you pissed off has a lot of resources," I tell her. "Government, police, or organized crime. They had to canvas every hotel in greater New Orleans for a girl matching your description."

Ellie's sharp. "Including this one?"

"Maybe. It depends if they found yours first. I don't think they've been here, but there's nothing to stop them from starting over. This time they'll search for a couple matching *our* description."

"We're not safe here."

"No, but I think we have a little time."

"But Rowan might not."

"I don't think they're government or police," I say. "That leaves organized crime."

I get to my feet. "It's late. Hit the sack, we'll start first thing in the morning."

The rain hasn't let up. Fortunately, there are staircases to the second floor behind the office and coffee shop. I see Ellie to her room, then go around the second-floor balcony to mine. Lock the door, collapse into an easy chair.

Wind is lashing the rain against the windows. The droplets are drumming against the roof like BB shot.

I stare at my phone, punch a speed dial.

"Breed." Stein picks up at the first ring. "How's New Orleans?"

Alright, I'm impressed. "How do *you* know where I am?"

"Only *you* can kill a man with a drinking straw."

"Doesn't word get around."

"Your footprints were all over it. Speed, surprise, violence of action… and always, a touch of creativity." A mattress creaks as Stein rolls over in bed. It's well after midnight. "Who's the girl?"

"The CIA doesn't know everything."

"I want to hear it from you."

"Ellie. She messaged me."

"That figures. She missed a call with her handler. Why?"

I start at the beginning and tell Stein everything I know. "She and her sister have run into a very bad lot. I'm going to send you the files Ellie stole. Her sister and a dead boy named Bailey. A surveillance video. It shows a man and a woman kidnapping Rowan. Your team should be able to enhance the images. Maybe get positive IDs."

"Alright. Why don't you go to the police and show them the video? It's evidence against Calthorpe and this handyman."

"I don't think they're the brains. If the police sweat them

and they clam up, we may never find Rowan. From what Ellie says, they don't know that we have the video. Ellie got a look at some paper files, but those are just health checkups."

"You know medical records are private. Those kids have a right to privacy."

"Which they surrendered when they applied to stay at Miriam Winslet. It sounds perfectly reasonable for a shelter to check abused and trafficked kids for STDs and diseases related to IV drug use. The cameras and security measures at the house make sense to prevent kids from using drugs on the premises."

"Breed, you'd make a great defense attorney."

"Just trying to think like the other side. Have some doctors look through those files and see if they notice anything. Tomorrow, Ellie and I are going to learn all we can about Bailey. Whatever happened to him may give us clues to Rowan's situation."

"You know she could be dead."

"Of course. But I assume nothing. Neither does Ellie."

6

DAY TWO - STORYVILLE, 0800 HRS

People tend to associate the French Quarter with Bourbon Street. Those same people also associate Storyville, New Orleans' famous red-light district, with the French Quarter. In fact, the Storyville that existed in 1917 was an area north of the French Quarter, east of Iberville and north of Rampart.

I step from my room onto the balcony. Pluck a hair, lick it, and stick it high on my door and doorjamb. I'm going to be gone most of the day, and I want to know if I've had visitors while I'm away.

There's no question Ellie and I are in danger. Whoever found her first hotel has the capacity to find us at this one. Having said that, I don't know any place in town safer. We can move again, of course. I'm prepared to do that, but want to play things by ear.

Ellie and I meet at the hotel coffee shop. The flagstones in the courtyard are shiny and wet from last night's rain, and the air smells damp and fresh. We have a good breakfast, then walk to Canal Street. Take a streetcar up to Basin Street, and get off in Storyville. The area is nowhere near as picturesque or atmospheric as the Quarter. The buildings are more widely spaced and look commercial.

There it is. The *Storyville Gazette*, once a third-tier print publication, now a second-tier online publication. A dingy front, like many of the businesses in this part of New Orleans.

I'm a bit surprised to find a receptionist. "We're here to see Robert Garnier," I say.

"Do you have an appointment?"

"Afraid not. We won't take much of his time, if he'd be so kind as to see us."

"Give me a moment." The receptionist gets up and walks down a corridor lined with offices. Pokes her head into one of them.

We did our research over breakfast. Found an article written two months ago about the death of Bailey Mitchell, seventeen years old, formerly a guest at the Miriam Winslet Shelter. The story had been reported by Robert Garnier of the *Storyville Gazette*.

The receptionist looks back our way, catches my eye, and waves us over. We walk down the corridor. Most of the offices are empty, but there are a couple of people opening up their laptops and sipping their morning coffee. These are the early birds. Apparently, Robert Garnier is one of those.

"Mr. Garnier? I'm Breed. This is my niece, Mary Louise Kennan."

Garnier, a trim young man in his early thirties, stands to shake hands. "Call me Robert."

The receptionist leaves us with the writer. The office is too small to fit two chairs in front of his writing desk. I motion for Ellie to take the chair, and I stand by the door.

"How can I help you?" Garnier asks.

"We're looking for information on a boy named Bailey Mitchell. He was found dead in a swamp a couple of months ago. You wrote the story."

"I did. There wasn't much to it, I'm afraid. The boy stayed at the Miriam Winslet Shelter for Homeless and Trafficked Children for six months. He left one day without checking out. The staff searched for him, called the police. The police weren't too fussed about it. These runaways come and go all the time. A week later, a body floated up in the Resurrection Parish swamp. The sheriff identified the deceased as Bailey Mitchell."

Ellie and I exchange glances. "Resurrection Parish?"

"Yes, it's a small parish west of Orleans and Jefferson. Why?"

"The guests at Miriam Winslet receive free healthcare at Resurrection General."

"That's some kind of coincidence."

"There *are* no coincidences," I tell him. "What was the cause of death?"

"Blood loss."

"You don't sound convinced."

"I'm not. They wanted the murder to go away. I'm the only writer who covered the story. When I tried to follow up, I received no cooperation. As far as I know, the case is still open, but the authorities have dropped it down a memory hole."

Garnier gets up, goes to a set of filing cabinets. The drawers are labeled by year. He slides open the current year's cabinet and searches for a file.

"Hardcopy is still useful," he says. "Some photographs, hand sketches don't digitize well. I keep both digital and paper files. You'd be surprised how much is in the paper files."

There's a photograph of a teenage boy with short brown hair, a thin face and a troubled countenance. He couldn't seem to look into the camera, giving his features a heavy-lidded expression.

Another photograph shows a clearing, a kind of muddy beach next to a swamp. Bald cypress trees in the background and to one side. Yellow police tape stretched between poles. Police stand aside as ambulance attendants carry a misshapen bundle away on a stretcher.

"No photos of the body?"

"None. They wouldn't let me get any closer than that. Shooed me off."

Garnier spreads a hand-drawn map on the table. He points to the southern edge of a large body of water, Lake Pontchartrain. "This shaded crescent below the lake is all swamp and marshland," he says. "I-10 is raised above the marsh and leads west once you get past the airport."

"*All* of that is swamp?"

"Swamp and marsh. There's a difference. Swampland has partially submerged trees. Marsh is reeds and grass. You can see where you get solid ground, to the sides of the crescent. Especially toward Lake Maurepas. There's boating on Lake Pontchartrain, and pleasure boats moored in those areas where there isn't much marsh. In the marshy areas south of I-10, you need to use airboats because submerged screws foul in the reeds regardless of a boat's draft."

I did time in the swamps of Florida during Ranger School, so I understand the distinction he's making.

"There's no serious construction until you are well inland. This is not exactly prime lakefront property. In fact, there were a few buildings in there. Low-rent public housing, fishing cabins and such. Hurricane Katrina flooded the place and washed it all away. Since then, they've rebuilt some of the public housing because there was no place else to put it. And if those people get flooded out again, who cares?"

"You're not serious."

"I don't think that way, but there are people who do. The body was found here." Garnier points to a small X at the edge of the swamp. He's drawn a road from Resurrection to the south. A bit farther west along the edge of the swamp is a small rectangle.

"I take it you have to drive up from Resurrection because the site is inaccessible from the highway."

"That's right." Garnier pushes the photograph next to the map. "You see here, to the right in the photo. It looks like a rotten pier. People used to fish off there. Farther to the right, outside the image, you'll find gator traps."

"Alligators!" Ellie exclaims.

Garnier looks up at the child. "Yeah. Alligators. They come up onto the banks, so watch out. There are pythons, too. The bigger pythons can actually kill gators."

Ellie stares wide-eyed. "Pythons."

The writer smiles. "Yeah, pythons are becoming the apex predator in these swamps. Hurricane Andrew destroyed a breeding facility in 1992, and they got loose in the bayou. They've been breeding ever since. Katrina scattered them *everywhere*. Just this year, the Department of Wildlife and Fisheries removed a fifteen-foot reticulated python and a three-foot ball python from the French Quarter. I covered those stories. Actually pumped up tourist interest."

"You're kidding."

"No, it was a thing during Mardi Gras. Some people keep snakes as pets. Love to drape them over their shoulders, sit with them on the sofa. Great until the pet gets to be twenty feet long. Then they dump them in the swamp. It's illegal to own pythons over eight feet long unless you have a permit."

Ellie shudders. "So I can keep a three-foot python?"

"Apparently so. Come to think of it, I should research the statute and do another story. I'll bet it says you have to destroy them when they reach eight feet."

I think back to Ranger School and our training in the swamps. "It's the moccasins and copperheads you want to watch out for," I say. "What's this rectangle here, west of the X?"

"That's Resurrection Bayou—public housing. A bad joke, really. After Katrina, you couldn't give that land away. Instead, they built a slum."

"How nice." I raise my phone. "Can I take a picture of that?"

"Be my guest."

I compose a close-up of the map, capture a photo. "Did they find the boy's family?"

"No, and no one stepped forward. I will say this—there was another girl found dead in the swamp well over a year ago. I didn't cover that story, and it was memory-holed too."

Ellie furrows her brow. "You think this could be, like... a serial killer?"

Garnier turns to Ellie. "I didn't say that. This is the first time I've thought about it. In Vegas the mob buries bodies in the desert. In New Orleans, they bury them in the swamp."

The writer looks thoughtful. Turns back to me. "Why are *you* so interested?"

"A girl went missing from Miriam Winslet last week. I'm a friend of the family, and they asked me to look into it."

"In what capacity?"

"As a friend of the family. The girl and her parents are estranged. Let's say the family relationships are complicated."

"Given the Miriam Winslet mission statement, that goes with the territory."

"Exactly. Do you have archives? How can we find out if other teens have gone missing or been found murdered?"

"We've been digitizing our archives ever since the lockdowns. We have a room in the back where you can log in and search them. The digitized material goes back five years. That's when we converted from a paper outlet to an online outlet. The paper archives go back much further, but they occupy two full rooms in the back."

"Can we examine them? I'd especially like to see what you have on the other girl."

"Register online, and I'll make sure you're approved." Garnier gets up, goes to the door, and calls the receptionist. "Donna, please show them the archives reading room."

"Thank you." I shake Garnier's hand. "You've been very helpful."

"Whatever you find, you let me know."

"Of course."

The receptionist leads us farther down the hall to a small room at the very back. Sitting on a desk is an ancient desktop PC. The website for the archive is written on a piece of paper and taped to the monitor. "Free to use," the girl says, and leaves us to our research.

I hold the chair for Ellie. "This is where we divide up the labor."

"What do you mean?"

"I want you to stay here and look for the story on that girl from a year ago. Then look for any other disappearances or murders that could be related. Go back five years to start."

"The serial killer theory."

"If it is a serial killer, we have a pretty good idea who *they* are. But I think there's more to it than that, don't you?"

"I guess so. Serial killers work alone, don't they?"

"Not all the time. But no serial killer is going to send six guys to kidnap you out of a diner."

"Guess not. What will you be doing?"

"I'm going to rent a car and check out the site where Bailey was found."

7

DAY TWO - RESURRECTION PARISH, 1000 HRS

The Bayou Road to the swamp is little more than a goat trail. Cypress trees festooned with Spanish moss crowd it on both sides. I drive the Hertz Audi A4 down the middle and pull over to let an old Kia Spectra pass going the other way. A haggard mother is at the wheel and scruffy kids are hanging out the rear passenger windows.

The road opens up to a clearing looking onto the swamp. There's the rotten pier, exactly as Garnier described it. The trees droop gracefully. Spanish moss hangs to the water and tangles with the reeds that stab from the surface. In the distance, a cloudy sky glowers over the gray waters of Lake Pontchartrain.

I park off the road and climb out. Walk down to the water. The red earth is smooth and undisturbed. Two months ago, this place had been torn up by police and emergency vehicles. Trampled by dozens of men. Garnier's photo showed yellow tape and a police line, but it didn't look like the scene had been properly secured.

My eyes quarter the ground. Past the pier, a structure that looks like a gibbet sticks up out of the water. A chain hangs from the end, terminating in a hook that has been stuck into a kind of waterfowl. The bait hangs two feet above the surface of the water.

Gator trap.

The air is filled with a cacophony of honking and bird calls. In the distance, a skein of ducks skims the surface of the lake. I'm surprised by the expanse of lake and sky, the sweep of the beach.

I imagine the boy's body floating half submerged among the reeds. Who found it? The story didn't say.

Two hundred yards farther, along the waterline, I come to the remains of a bonfire. I approach, and a swarm of flies takes flight. Much of the loose charcoal was washed away by last night's heavy rain. But there are still some blackened sticks a couple of feet long. And scarcely recognizable shapes, giving off an ungodly stench.

I go to one knee and pick up a stick. Twelve inches unburned and another six inches of charcoal. I scrape the charred black end of the stick with a thumbnail. It has not been freshly carbonized. I use the stick to poke at a blackened ball. Roll it over. One end is a stump with charred black tubes sticking out. There's a charred dowel planted in the mess. Roll it over again. It's a burned cat's head. Too heavy to wash into the swamp. Someone stuck a dowel into the stump of its neck and planted it in the ground to hold the head up. When the dowel burned, the head fell over.

Can't find the cat's body. But over there is something that looks like a blackened Thanksgiving dinner. It's the charred body of a headless chicken. Burst from the heat, spilling burned gizzards.

Damn, the flies are coming back. I get to my feet, take out my phone, and snap a photo of the fire, the cat's head, and the body of the chicken.

When was the fire built? Certainly after the boy's body was found. Not last night, because it was raining. But not too long ago, judging from the remains. I estimate forty-eight hours.

Bailey Mitchell. Death by stabbing? There's no guarantee he was killed here. The body could have been dumped into the lake and floated here. Somehow, I don't think so. This doesn't have to be the only fire built on this spot. I need to see the police report.

"What you doing here, boy?"

Turn, check out the two men who've approached me from behind. The soft earth cushioned their footsteps. Big, beefy guys. They look like Cajun heavies. One of them wears a long, shaggy red beard. The other is black-haired and clean-shaven. The clean-shaven guy is wearing farmer's coveralls that make him look like a country bumpkin. The bearded guy is wearing dark pants, a dirty T-shirt, and a red-and-black plaid work shirt.

The bearded guy is carrying a three-foot wooden club. The bumpkin's carrying an axe handle.

In the distance, a battered Ford F-150 pickup stands parked in front of my Audi. The distance and cacophony of swamp birds kept me from hearing the truck's approach.

Another man stands next to the driver's door. He's leaning casually against the truck, enjoying the show. The cargo bed draws my attention. A big black pit bull is standing alert, with his forepaws on the cargo bed rail. He's panting and slobbering all over the side of the pickup. Nice.

"Stopped to look around," I say.

"Ain't nothing to see here, boy." Thick accent. Old French and English. Cajun.

It will be hard work, but I can take the two guys. Leaving number three back at the truck was a mistake. Three-on-one would be a much harder ask. The dog is the problem. He's a brute, and he'll be hard to stop.

Maybe if I get my hands on that club, I can beat the dog to death.

"I heard a boy was found dead here about two months ago. Can you tell me anything about it?"

"Shit." Red Beard spits. "You don't listen too good. This is our land, boy. We don't like people poking around, and we sure don't like people asking questions about dead boys."

"I'll be going, then."

Circle around Red Beard, start walking back to the car. Hard for me to keep an eye on all of them. Well, ears are important too.

I hear a swish of clothing as Red Beard turns to swing the club at me. Aiming at my head. I duck low, and the bat flashes past, missing by an inch.

He should have gone for my legs. A good move that would destroy all but the best opponents.

But Red Beard went for my head, the easiest attack to avoid. The momentum of his two-handed swing carried his center of gravity well over to his left. I step to his right and chop the edge of my right hand against the right side of his neck. Kick his leg out from under him. He goes down hard, and I take the club from him as he falls.

Bumpkin steps in with the axe handle raised, but I turn and hold the club like a rifle at port arms. A flexible position from which I can jab with the blunt end, use the club to parry blows, strike at his throat, or step back and swing it like a bat.

The dog is barking. I glance left. It's still in the cargo bed of the truck. The driver looks like he's trying to make up his mind what to do.

I stare down Bumpkin. "Back off," I tell him. "No one's hurt yet."

Red Beard struggles to his feet. Looks like he wants to rush me.

There's an electronic whoop—a short blast from a police siren.

A blue-and-white police cruiser approaches from the direction of Resurrection Bayou. Pulls over and stops in front of the pickup. A woman's voice issues from a loudspeaker.

"Bastien," the woman calls. "Rémy. That's enough. You boys go home now, or I'll take you in."

Bumpkin and Red Beard scowl.

The woman's electronically amplified voice echoes over the beach. "Clear off, boys, or there will be trouble."

The Cajuns straighten. Cowed, they start back toward their truck.

I call to Red Beard. "Hey."

The Cajuns turn to me, and I hold the club out to Red Beard. He looks at me with suspicion, reaches forward and takes it. "Expect me to say thank you?"

I lock eyes with the Cajun. "I don't expect you to say anything."

The men walk to their truck. They stare at the police cruiser with resentment and cram themselves into the pickup's cab. The dog's stopped barking. The engine roars to life, and they drive toward Resurrection Bayou.

A woman gets out of the police cruiser. She's wearing

dark brown pants, a light khaki shirt and a gold badge. A pistol belt with holster, Taser, folding baton and cuffs. She reaches into the car and takes out a wide-brimmed sheriff's hat. Sets it on her head.

I walk to the police cruiser. The cop is in her late thirties, with strong features. That's a way of saying she's not beautiful, but attractive. After all, who needs beautiful?

"Who are you?" she asks.

"I'm Breed."

"You got a first name?"

"Yes."

She stares at me for a full second. Snorts. "Let's see some ID."

I reach for my hip pocket and slowly take out my wallet with two fingers. Hand it to her. She shakes her head. "Take the card out and hand it to me."

Lady's not about to tie up her hands fumbling with my wallet. I take out my armed forces card and hand it to her. She examines it carefully, then hands it back.

"Well, *former* chief warrant officer Breed, what are *you* doing in *my* parish?"

"A girl went missing from the Miriam Winslet Shelter in New Orleans a few days ago. Her family asked me to find her. I heard a young boy from the same home was found out here."

"How come her family didn't come to get her?"

"Not her parents. Her sister."

"That makes a bit of sense," the woman says. "Breed, you have no standing. That means because you're not family, you have no right to go poking around."

"I understand that, Sheriff..."

"Kennedy. Breed, you have no standing."

"Can I show you something else, Sheriff Kennedy?"

"You may."

I remove another card from my wallet and hand it to her. It's a plain white card with Stein's number. A variation of the cards special operators are given to use if they run into trouble. "Call that number," I tell her, "and all will be made clear."

"You wait here."

Sheriff Kennedy walks around her cruiser, stands twenty feet away. Takes out her phone and calls Stein. The two converse for five minutes. Kennedy refuses to take her eyes off me. When she ends the call, her features soften. She squeezes the phone into her hip pocket.

"Witness protection." The sheriff shakes her head.

"Yes. Rowan Miller's sister. Rowan's been abused. She was going to join her sister when everything went pear-shaped."

"My department received the bulletin on Rowan Miller. We haven't been able to find her."

"Will you help?"

"I'll do what I can."

8

DAY TWO - RESURRECTION PARISH, 1100 HRS

Sheriff Kennedy invites me to sit together in her car. She climbs in behind the wheel and I get in front next to her. The cruiser's mobile data terminal and keyboard are mounted to the dash between us. The interior is soaked in the smell of grease and synthetic upholstery that I find common to government vehicles.

I slide the passenger seat back and stretch my legs. "Please, tell me about Bailey Mitchell."

The sheriff tells me how she was called to Resurrection Bayou two months ago. "I've never seen anything like it," Kennedy says, "and I hope I never do again."

BAILEY MITCHELL WASN'T a body when they found him. He was *remains*. He'd been found by Cajuns from Resurrection Bayou. Naked and gutted like a fish. His shell was found floating in the swamp. One-third was washed up on the land.

Two-thirds were submerged in swamp water, hidden among the reeds.

The boy had been eviscerated. Opened up from pelvis to collarbone. His sternum had been removed and his ribs had been snapped off and discarded. His bowels and all the internal organs had been removed. The interior of his body was literally scraped clean. Swamp water washed in and out of the hollow shell. The lips of the sac opened and closed as the deputies and ambulance attendants manipulated his limbs to pull him onto the beach.

Kennedy swallowed the taste of bile. She thought she and her deputies had seen everything. They'd seen a woman hit by a motorcycle, ripped in half and disemboweled. Seen a man with his face blown off by a shotgun at three feet. Seen one baby cooked alive in an oven, another boiled alive in a cooking pot. Nothing could make her deputies whup their cookies, but what had been done to Bailey Mitchell came close.

She looked down at the naked shell. The boy's male apparatus was gone. The musculature of his arms and legs was intact. The musculature of his belly and lower back had been carved away. Only his spine and hips kept his legs connected to the rest of his body. It was like he had been gutted for a hideous feast.

Then, there was the fire. Twenty feet away from the body, a great bonfire had been built. It was still smoking, and the embers glowed. The fire had been used to burn the boy's organs.

KENNEDY SWALLOWS HARD, puts her hand to her throat and looks away. I've seen that look before. People get that when they recall the stench of burned flesh. The kind of smell that clogs your nose and makes you gag. Smell you can taste.

I talked to a therapist about it at the VA. When I returned from combat, sights made me smell things. Smells made me taste things. Things I touched made me smell things. All from experiences in the field. The therapist explained *synesthesia* to me, the merging of senses. Not that I could fix it. But understanding it might help.

What she saw and smelled that day would stay with Sheriff Kennedy the rest of her life.

"Was it a ritual killing?" I ask.

"It had the look."

"Voodoo."

Kennedy looks toward the dark discoloration where the fire had burned. "There's New Orleans Voodoo," she says. "It's called *Obeah*. Elsewhere, *Santeria*. Same thing. It is practiced, but they don't do human sacrifice."

"Really. There's a bonfire over there, two days old. Much of it's been washed away by last night's rain, but someone burned a dead cat's head and a headless chicken. There are some other remains mixed in I don't recognize. I have no idea why they kept the cat's head and the chicken's body."

Kennedy looks toward the cold fire. "I'll take your word for it."

"Did you investigate *Santeria* practitioners in connection with the Mitchell murder?"

"We considered it."

"How seriously?"

"Seriously, but cautiously. Breed, the First Amendment guarantees people's right to establish religion and practice it freely. I have no right to interrogate people about religious practices. The Supreme Court has been very firm, very explicit about this constitutional issue."

"Even when practicing that religion involves human sacrifice?"

Kennedy adopts a testy tone. "I said we considered it."

I give up. "There was another case. A girl, a year before Bailey Mitchell."

The sheriff looks at me from across the police car. "You've been a busy boy."

"I try to keep moving. Tell me about her."

"Her name was Taylor Purdy. She was found by the swamp, just like Bailey. Half a mile down the road near Resurrection Bayou. Everything about the scene was the same. Gutted like a fish. Sternum and ribs removed. Her uterus and ovaries were gone. Another bonfire, all her organs burned. There was *one* difference."

"What was that?"

"She'd just undergone a keyhole appendectomy at Resurrection General. She was being kept overnight for release the following day. She sneaked out of the hospital without being released. She was found three days later."

"You've got two ritualistic murders and three disappearances."

"It would seem so," Kennedy says. "In the cases of Mitchell and Purdy, the bodies were found three days after they went missing."

"Rowan Miller has been missing two days."

Kennedy shakes her head. "Two data points are not enough to determine a pattern."

"Two points make a straight line," I tell her. "Now I have a few things to share with you."

Sharing information develops trust. Kennedy can help me. I tell her as much as I dare about Ellie and what Ellie found at Miriam Winslet. I don't tell her about the video Ellie took from Victoria Calthorpe's computer. Then I tell her about the six men who attacked us in the Quarter.

"The NOPD are looking for you."

"People have terrible powers of observation. They'll come up with half a dozen different descriptions."

"That's exactly what they've got," Kennedy says. "Seems everybody's attention was focused on all the broken bodies you left behind. Now tell me why I shouldn't arrest you."

"Because I'm one of the good guys."

I FOLLOW Sheriff Kennedy's cruiser toward Resurrection General. She pointed out that I had no standing. That meant I couldn't show up at the hospital's doorstep and start asking questions about Rowan, Bailey, and Taylor Purdy. The cases were open, so she agreed to go with me.

On the way to the hospital, I call Ellie.

"Have you found anything?" Ellie asks.

"Yes, a fair bit about Bailey Mitchell."

"I found the girl who was killed a year ago."

"Taylor Purdy."

"That's her," Ellie says. "I found the story in the digital archive. She didn't disappear from Miriam Winslet. She disappeared from Resurrection General."

Exactly as Sheriff Kennedy described. "Anything else?"

"Nothing much. She was admitted for appendicitis. Had routine surgery, the kind they do with fiber-optic tubes. She was scheduled to be released the next day, but disappeared without being checked out."

"Is that all?"

"There wasn't much."

"Okay, ask Robert Garnier who wrote the story. Look for paper notes. The body was found in the swamp near Resurrection Bayou. It's a public housing development. Find a map, a description of where the body was found."

"I'll try."

"If you can't find a map, talk to the reporter who wrote the story. Ask him to describe the place for you and draw your own map. Have you found anybody else?"

"Not yet, still looking."

"Put that on hold for now. Find the map. You have time because I have to take a rain check on lunch."

"Breed, I'm hurt."

"Don't be. I'll make it up to you at dinner. The sheriff is taking me to Resurrection General. I'm going to meet people and ask some questions."

"How did you manage that?"

"I'll tell you tonight. While you're doing research, find out all you can about Voodoo. *Santeria* and *Obeah*. *Obeah* is New Orleans Voodoo."

"What's that got to do with anything?"

"Somebody is practicing Voodoo on the site where Bailey Mitchell's body was found."

"This is too weird."

"One last thing. Don't go back to the hotel without me."

"Why not?"

"Because those people who tried to grab you yesterday are still looking for us."

I disconnect the call. Sheriff Kennedy signals a right turn

as she pulls onto the road that leads to Resurrection General.

What we have here are three disappearances, all tied to Miriam Winslet. Two murders, found in the same stretch of swamp. Resurrection General, a hospital that serviced all three teenagers.

There are no coincidences.

When we arrive at the hospital, Sheriff Kennedy asks for the nurse coordinating the relationship with Miriam Winslet. Reception pages Nurse Karen Shelly. Kennedy and the nurse know each other. The sheriff introduces me, and I explain what I want.

Nurse Shelly looks puzzled. "Of course, I'll help any way I can," she says, "but I've been through this before with the sheriff."

"It can't hurt to have a fresh pair of eyes look at things," Kennedy says. "Mr. Breed has an interest as a friend of Rowan Miller's family."

"But Rowan Miller hasn't been killed."

Shelly's objection is disingenuous. No one with two brain cells to rub together could miss the connection between the three cases.

My tone is pointed. "Not yet."

"Very well." Shelly is reluctant, and it shows. She reaches under the nursing station's counter, picks up a tablet, and activates its touch screen. The device brings up some Resurrection General wallpaper. She taps the screen to display a login prompt. I can see a single field and a request to enter the user's PIN. There's no need for a user ID. When she logs in, the system automatically associates her unique PIN with the device.

I can't believe how many credit card companies still require four-digit PINs. Ditto banking machines. They're easy to guess if you can see one or two numbers entered. That's why banks advise you to always shield your PIN.

Shelly turns the back of the tablet toward me. Taps four numbers in rapid succession. She's facing me, so I can't see the digital keypad, but I *can* see the pattern her fingers make. She taps twice on the upper left of the pad—my right, because I'm facing her. She taps in the middle. Finally she taps once at the lower right—my left. That means she probably typed 1-1-5-9. Maybe 1-1-5-8. Too easy.

Shelly hands me the tablet. "All our records are online. We can see the records of Rowan Miller, Bailey Mitchell and Taylor Purdy right here."

The nurse leans close and taps on an icon labeled *Patient Records*. There's a list of names and a search bar on top.

"Isn't it a little risky leaving these lying around?" I ask. The tablets are ubiquitous. Everybody has one.

"They're connected to the hospital network," Shelly says. "All the data is in our cloud. Take the device one step outside the hospital and it goes offline. Nothing is stored on the device, so it becomes a paperweight."

I tap "Bailey Mitchell" into the search box, and the list of names is automatically reduced to one.

"Is there a place we can sit down?" I ask. "It would be helpful if you walk us through these charts and explain what's going on."

"Of course. Let's find a conference room."

Shelly leads us down a corridor. There's a small conference room at the end, with a table that seats eight. There's a large flatscreen mounted on the wall. The nurse turns it on and draws another smaller tablet from the pocket of her lab coat. The one I'm holding is about 8½" by 11" in size. Hers is about 5" by 7", the size of a paperback book. She logs in and mirrors her own tablet's screen to the TV.

I glance at the tablet she loaned me, and it's still working. That's useful information—a user can be logged into two devices at once.

"Let's start with Rowan's file," she says. "You'll find they are all laid out the same."

The nurse starts with the questionnaires. I feel like I've heard it all before, because Ellie gave me a thorough briefing, and I saw the file she stole from Calthorpe's laptop. Shelly speaks of the need to obtain a thorough medical history, details of current and previous drug use, childhood diseases, STDs, and diseases associated with intravenous drug use.

"The questionnaires provide an oral history," Shelly says. "We then cross-check with laboratory tests. We also search for other diseases that the patient may not know about."

"Such as?"

"Inherited diseases, for instance. From a buccal swab, we obtain squamous cells and perform a karyotype. Chromosomes tell a fascinating story."

"Of course."

"We take several buccal swabs. We can test for various cancer markers. Those are listed here, and Rowan is negative for all."

Page after page of test data scroll past. When she has finished, Shelly says, "I can leave you to look at the others on your own."

"Taylor Purdy was different in one respect," I say.

Shelly looks surprised. "Really?"

"Yes. Neither Rowan Miller nor Bailey Mitchell were admitted to the hospital. Taylor Purdy was admitted for appendicitis."

"Of course." Shelly looks embarrassed. "I'd forgotten. There's a separate section here for Purdy's pre-op and post-op examinations."

"What were the electrocardiograms and echocardiograms for?"

"Examinations for congenital heart disease. Valve function. Tests for our electricians and plumbers, we like to say." At that, the charming Nurse Shelly smiles. "The hospital is providing its services to Miriam Winslet guests free of charge, but the hospital remains liable and exposed to potential litigation if anything goes wrong or is missed. We do not cut corners in the case of charity work. If anything, we have to be exceptionally thorough."

"These are the patient records," I say. "Where are the autopsy reports?"

Shelly hesitates. "They're in a different sub-folder."

"May we see them," Kennedy says. It's not a request.

The nurse fusses with her tablet. She calls up Bailey Mitchell's file and displays the autopsy report.

The medical details mean nothing to me. My purpose in asking to see the report was to make sure it was there and procedures were followed. Shelly scrolls through pages of medical terminology, comes to a set of detailed color photographs.

I have seen corpses. Men who were shot to death and men blown in half by artillery. The images of the children, laid open on the autopsy table, are more horrible than anything I've ever seen. The only thing missing is the sickening stench of death one encounters on the battlefield.

The boy is barely recognizable. Kennedy described Bailey Mitchell's body as having been eviscerated like a fish. These photos are appalling. Large flaps of muscle had been carved out of the abdomen and the small of the back. Attachment to the spine is all that holds the pitiful thing together. Nurse Shelly looks visibly ill.

I've seen the same thing hundreds of times, hunting deer. Once a hunter's brought the animal down, he has to prepare it. Skin the carcass, cut it open, remove the entrails, and pack the edible meat for his freezer. The horror—this butcher had taken his knife to a child. Hadn't bothered to skin him. The damage to the ribs and sternum was gratuitous. When preparing a deer, the contents of the chest cavity can be removed from below. The killer enjoyed his work.

"Let's see Taylor Purdy."

I want to see Purdy, but I also want to keep Nurse Shelly focused on practical tasks. These images are more disturbing than those even a surgical nurse is exposed to. And I don't think Shelly is a surgical nurse.

The girl's body was butchered, but not as thoroughly destroyed as the boy's. Most of Taylor Purdy's musculature is intact though she was eviscerated in much the same way.

"What was the cause of death?"

"Exsanguination."

"What does that mean?"

"She bled to death."

"What about the boy?"

Shelly taps on her tablet's touch keyboard. Recalls Bailey Mitchell's report and scrolls to the cause of death. "Same."

"Can we speak to the pathologist who performed the autopsies?"

"Dr. Durand." Shelly glances at Kennedy. "The sheriff has already spoken to him."

"Humor me," I say.

"I don't know if he's available."

"Please check." Kennedy's tone is firm.

Nurse Shelly lifts her phone, has the doctor paged.

While we wait for the doctor to arrive, I ask, "Can we have a copy of the autopsy reports?"

"I'm afraid not." Shelly seems genuinely outraged. "These are not to leave the hospital."

I want Stein to have one of her pathologists examine the reports. This could be a problem.

The door to the conference room opens, and a sharp-featured man in a white lab coat enters the room. Shelly, relieved to be drawn away from the autopsy reports, introduces him as Dr. Emile Durand.

The doctor has long, thin fingers and impossibly soft skin. He applies the faintest pressure before releasing my hand. Stares at me through round, wire-framed glasses under a crown of curly black hair. He does not seem inquisitive or puzzled by our summons. He is only... present.

"How can I help?" he asks. "I have already spoken about these matters with Sheriff Kennedy."

"Humor me, Doctor. I find it's always best to hear a story firsthand."

"What do you want to know?"

Durand's voice is neutral. His manner is clinical, devoid of interest or speculation.

"How did Mitchell and Purdy die?"

"They died the same way. Massive blood loss. Their injuries were not survivable."

"That means they were alive when this was done to them."

"Yes. The injuries were inflicted from the area of the genitals and progressed to the chest cavity. Death did not occur until late in the process."

"Were they conscious?"

"It's not clear they were conscious when the injuries occurred."

"So they were anaesthetized."

"I didn't say that. Unconsciousness does not require anesthesia. They could have fainted early in the procedure."

I lift an eyebrow. "The *procedure*? Isn't that an odd word to use to describe what was done to these children?"

Durand wrinkles his nose. "How would *you* describe it?"

"Butchery."

The doctor says nothing.

"The boy's body suffered more destruction than the girl's. Why do you think that was?"

"I don't know," Durand says. "The major damage occurred postmortem. The chest cavity and the large musculature."

Durand is hopeless. He's wrapped up in technical issues. For him, these were simple laboratory exercises. Two children were eviscerated and died in the process. No medical mystery to tweak his intellectual curiosity. A simple case, open and shut.

"Thank you, Doctor."

Durand sticks his pampered hands in his pockets and walks out without another word.

I turn to Nurse Shelly, hand her the tablet she gave me at the station. "May we see Taylor Purdy's room?"

"Of course. I'll have to find out which one it was."

"Please."

Shelly takes us to the third floor. We step out of the elevator and the doors suck shut behind us. There are two sets of big butterfly doors on either side of the hall, labeled *North 3* and *South 3*. The nurse leads us into *North 3*.

A cheery greeting from the staff at the nursing station. The ward seems quiet, there are only a handful of people on the floor. We walk down the corridor on the left. Families are visiting with patients. Sitting at their bedsides, chatting.

Taylor Purdy occupied the second room from the end. Currently vacant. The hospital bed has been made, and the room is spotless. The windows are polished and offer a view of a pristine, oak-shaded park, where other patients take their morning walks.

I go to the window, slide it open and lean out. Drink in the fresh air.

"Lovely," I say.

As I thought, the modern lines of the hospital have the windows flush with the outer walls. I close the window and turn to face Kennedy and Shelly. "Can we do a turn around the other side of the ward?"

"Of course."

A tall man steps into the room. Fiftyish, athletic and about my height. Dark hair, maybe colored, over olive skin and a wide smile. "Karen," he says, addressing Nurse Shelly, "I heard we have guests."

"Mark, how fortunate you're on-site today. You've met Sheriff Kennedy. This is Mr. Breed. Mr. Breed, this is Mark Luka. Resurrection General is his hospital."

Luka laughs self-deprecatingly. "It's a privilege to serve the community," he says. "Mr. Breed, what brings you to visit today?"

"I've been asked to help find Rowan Miller," I tell him. "I understand two other guests of Miriam Winslet have gone missing in the last year and turned up murdered. I'm rather concerned."

I fix Luka's eyes with mine. He doesn't miss a beat. "Resurrection General provides service to all Miriam Winslet guests. What they do once they leave the hospital is nothing to do with us, I'm afraid."

"Of course not," I say. "Taylor Purdy, however, disappeared from Resurrection General. That's why we thought to have another look."

"We're an open book, Mr. Breed. What else can we show you?"

"Mr. Breed wanted to tour the rest of the ward," Shelly says.

"Of course," Luka says. "Please lead the way."

Luka's manner has a certain old-world quality. I can't place his accent. It's Eastern European, but not quite. Maybe Northern Italy or Croatia.

"How long have you been in business?" I ask.

"You mean the hospital, I assume." Luka paces slowly beside me, hands behind his back. Love the way his suit drapes over his shoulders. Wonderful material. "About four years. The parish began construction, but ran into financial difficulty during the lockdowns. My development firm was involved in building the hospital, so we stepped in and carried the project in exchange for an equity stake. It's working out quite well."

"It must have been quite a risk, stepping into a new line of business."

"It was, Mr. Breed, but one's success depends on one's ability to calculate risk. I enjoy learning new businesses. It keeps me young."

Thirty minutes later, Kennedy and I emerge from the hospital and stroll to our cars.

"I gather you noticed everything I did when I first investigated Taylor Purdy's disappearance," Kennedy says.

"You mean that there was no way she could escape from that third-floor window? Or get past the nursing station unseen?"

"Unless it was very busy—"

"It's not busy at all."

"—or the station was unattended. I interviewed the nurses and reception clerks at the station, and it is always manned. Hospital policy."

"It's possible she snuck off," I say. "I once snuck away after an appendectomy."

"*You*? I don't believe it."

"I was on leave and had a date to see a show. I had keyhole surgery, just like Taylor. They were supposed to discharge me the next morning but couldn't find a doctor to sign off. By midafternoon, I decided I wasn't going to stand up my date and snuck away. Took her to the show, found a cab to take her home, and snuck back in. The hospital never noticed I was gone. Discharged me late that night."

Kennedy throws her head back and laughs. "You rascal. So it *is* possible."

We reach the cars, and I lean back against the Audi. Fold my arms. "It's possible, but Taylor Purdy did not sneak out of Resurrection General. You don't think so either."

The sheriff's face darkens. "No, Breed, I don't. But I also don't know where to go from here."

"Get me digital copies of the autopsy reports. I want to have Stein's pathologists review them. This hospital gives me the creeps."

"It's an unusual request because a verbal update from the pathologist has always been sufficient. I'll have to formally requisition them."

"Then it's best to get started."

"And what will *you* occupy yourself with?"

"I'm going to check on my research assistant."

THE AUDI HUMS ALONG I-10. I set my phone on handsfree and lay it on the passenger seat next to me. I thank Stein for interceding on my behalf with Sheriff Kennedy. Papers rustle in the background.

"Desmond Krainer," she says, "has a record. He served ten years in Angola for armed robbery. He and a couple of friends thought to knock over a liquor store. He was twenty-five, not the ringleader. He got off easy. When he got out, he drifted for a year, then got a job working for Miriam Winslet. He's been there ever since."

"Just the kind of guy you want around troubled kids."

"Great example. Victoria Calthorpe is a bit different. She has a master of education degree from Tulane. Got it online. Pretty routine career path. Started out as a teacher, then school administrator. Left her last position under a cloud. Don't know why, but I'm having it checked out. Anyway, she was hired by the Miriam Winslet Shelter five years ago."

"A year before Resurrection General commenced operations under new ownership."

"How did that happen?"

I tell Stein what I learned at the swamp and later at the hospital. "I think we should check out Mark Luka. He's too smooth by half. Some kind of property developer. Apparently he was contracted to build Resurrection General for the parish. Stepped in when they ran into financial difficulty. Now he owns it. Controlling interest or one hundred percent, I don't know."

"I'll check it out."

"This whole thing is getting messier by the minute," I say. "No question in my mind there's an organized crime aspect, but that doesn't stack with the Voodoo angle."

"No, it doesn't."

I think of Kennedy's description of Bailey Mitchell's corpse. "I'm thinking of getting Ellie out of this. It's going to get rough."

"How are you going to do that?"

"Put her on a bus."

"Like that's going to work."

I turn the Audi up Canal Street. "I have to go. Stay in touch."

"I FOUND ANOTHER GIRL," Ellie says.

"Show me."

I sit next to Ellie in the *Gazette*'s archive room. She's got a digitized story displayed on the computer screen. It shows the picture of a pretty Hispanic teenager with an open smile.

"Carmen Esposito, fifteen years old. She left the home three years ago and was killed in a hit-and-run."

"Not murdered in a swamp?"

"No, but it looks suspicious. The story says she left the Miriam Winslet Shelter and was hitching a ride upstate when she was hit by a car on Old US 51. It happened at night, the car didn't see her. She was killed."

"I agree it looks suspicious. Hold on."

I dial Sheriff Kennedy.

"Breed, what's up?"

"I have a name for you. Carmen Esposito, fifteen years old, three years ago. Left the Miriam Winslet Shelter and was killed by a hit-and-run while hitching north on Old US 51."

"I'll check it out."

"I want to see her files. Her medical records and her autopsy report."

"We don't even know that she was involved."

In that moment, I find myself absolutely certain that Carmen Esposito's death was not an accident. "She's involved."

I disconnect the call and turn back to Ellie. "Have you found any others?"

"Not yet."

"What about the map?"

"The guy who wrote the Taylor Purdy story is just down the corridor. Here's the paper file. There's no map, but he helped me sketch the scene."

Ellie spreads a piece of paper on the table. It's a simple drawing, but done to scale. There's a horizontal line showing the shore of the swamp. Little pencil strokes look like reeds. There are a series of rectangles and squares on the ground set back from the water. The buildings of Resurrection Bayou. A two-headed arrow indicates the buildings are a hundred and fifty yards from the water, separated by trees. The Bayou Road is drawn approaching from the east. An X marks the place Taylor Purdy's body was found, among the reeds at the water's edge.

The corner of a black-and-white photograph peeps from the corner of the file folder. I slide the photo onto the desktop. Taylor Purdy was a pretty, blond girl in her late teens with high, wide cheekbones and a bright smile.

I slide the photo back into the folder. "Anything on Voodoo?"

"I've found a couple of survey articles, but I haven't had a chance to read them. I get the feeling it's a kind of tourist thing. People come to see the city, so they feel they have to see a haunted house and buy some candles."

"I reckon it's a bit more than that to people who live here."

"Maybe. Probably better to speak to someone who knows about it."

Ellie's probably right, but we have to make do. "Okay. I'm going to go check out the Taylor Purdy site. See if you can find any more potential victims, but this time, limit your search to four years."

"Why four?"

"A hunch. Resurrection General opened its doors four years ago. Des Krainer was hired at Miriam Winslet four years ago. Victoria Calthorpe was hired five years ago. We have four known data points at three years, one year, six months, and…" I hesitate.

"Two days," Ellie says. "I know, Breed. I'm going crazy for Rowan. We *have* to find her."

9

DAY TWO - RESURRECTION BAYOU, 1400 HRS

I leave the Audi hidden deep in the woods, three hundred yards from Resurrection Bayou. I walk parallel to the road, just inside the tree line. I don't particularly want to run into Bastien, Rémy and their pit bull. At the same time, I'm not about to request a police escort to visit Resurrection Bayou.

The buildings look squalid. Six featureless, characterless brick blocks three stories high set in two rows. Each apartment has a set of windows set flush to the wall, a narrow private balcony, and sliding balcony doors. All the apartments look alike. The windows are open. Multicolored laundry has been draped over the balcony rails to dry.

A parking lot behind the second tier of buildings is open to the elements. Men and women are sitting on the balconies. The tenants in the second tier of buildings have no view of the water at all. Those in the front row have a view of the cypress trees in the first instance. Those on the top floor have their view of the swamp partially obscured by the treetops.

My eyes scan the parking lot, searching for any sign of Bastien and Rémy's pickup. It's not there. I step onto the road and cross to the trees separating the project from the swamp.

A group of kids runs past, shrieking and laughing. They disappear between the two rows of buildings. I make my way toward the swamp, brushing aside dangling ropes of Spanish moss. The salty scent of swamp water grows more pronounced the closer I get. Then I'm through the tree line and on the earthen beach.

It looks exactly like the earthen beach I saw this morning, half a mile east. No pier, no gator traps. I search for floating logs among the reeds. There are none.

I pick my way along the beach. The X Ellie drew on her sketch marked the place Taylor Purdy's body had been found. I imagine the girl, sliced open as Bailey Mitchell had been. Sternum removed, ribs snapped off, internal organs scooped out. The lips of the shell hanging open, breasts hanging flat to her sides.

There's no sign that a murder took place here. Fifty feet farther along, I see a dark patch of ground where fires have been built over months or years. I walk around it. There are no fresh signs. No half-burned sticks, no charcoal, no dead cats or headless chickens. The last fire built here went out long ago.

Disappointed, I turn and walk back into the trees.

I emerge in front of the first tier of buildings and walk east down the Bayou Road.

A black girl steps out of the last building in the front row and walks in my direction. She's carrying a big yellow shopping bag in her right hand. Thin, just this side of skinny. She's pretty, wearing a faded, flower-print shift that falls just past her knees. The breeze blows it against her slender limbs. The neck of the shift is open. She's wearing a plain white bra with narrow, stringy straps. Her hair is long, thick and wavy.

She's mixed-race. A wide mouth, thin lips, white teeth. Big, hazel eyes. She looks poor, and beautiful.

I greet her. "Hi, have you lived here long?"

She stops and looks me up and down. "That's an odd question, mister."

"I have my reasons for asking."

"I've lived here since they built the place after Katrina."

"You mean you were born here."

The girl smiles. "Not quite. My family moved to Resurrection Bayou when I was very young. I grew up here."

She's a bit over twenty.

"There was a girl killed over there by the swamp a year ago. Do you remember?"

The girl's face darkens. "I remember a lot of police."

"Did you see or hear anything the night before? The night before that?"

A shake of the head. Her eyes flick to the top floor, and the breeze blows twisted strands of hair across her eyes. She is lovely. "No, I didn't. Why do *you* care?"

When I met Sheriff Kennedy, I asked myself, *Who needs beautiful?* This girl is why you want beautiful. I'm looking at her eyes and seeing everything about her. She sees me looking, and she likes it.

Too bad she's lying.

Her glance at the top floor told me everything. She lives up there. She saw something that night, no question about it.

"A girl went missing from New Orleans a couple of days ago. Her family asked me to help find her. They're worried."

The girl's manner softens. "I'd help if I could, but I didn't see anything. Why does the girl matter?"

"Family thinks the same thing could happen to her."

I take a Hertz rental business card from my pocket. Scribble my name and phone number on the back and hand it to her. "I'm Breed."

The girl accepts the card and looks at both sides. Takes time to contemplate my handwriting. She doesn't want the conversation to end. "I'm Albertine."

"Albertine."

"Yeah." She flips the card over and over with her fingers.

"That's a beautiful name. You read Proust?"

Albertine breaks into a smile, and I want to drop down and go for it right there in the dust. She looks like she's thinking the same.

"I read *everything*," she says. "*You* don't look the type."

"What type is that?"

"The type to read Proust."

"*Albertine* was the only book of his I finished. I wanted to sleep with her."

Albertine bends over laughing. Her laughter tinkles in the breeze. "My God," she gasps, "who *are* you?"

I smile. "I have to get back to town. If you remember anything, call."

"I won't remember anything," she says. There's a wistful look in her eyes.

"Call anyway."

I walk back to my car. Before I duck into the tree line, I turn and look back. Bastien and Rémy have emerged from the project and are speaking with Albertine. I'd recognize that red beard and those bumpkin coveralls anywhere.

Bastien and Rémy argue with Albertine. They found me poking around the other beach. They left me with the sheriff. They're telling her I'm trouble. Albertine's back stiffens, and she shuts them up. No question the thin girl is in charge. She picks up her shopping bag and leads them through the cypress and toward the swamp.

That is curious.

I get into the Audi, slam the door, and start the engine. Pull onto the Bayou Road and head back toward Resurrection. When I reach the junction between the road to Resurrection and the I-10 on-ramp, I stop for the light.

To my right, a couple of hundred meters from the junction, squats a silver, late-model, Ford Mustang. Two men, shadowy figures, are in front, sitting very still. Their attention is focused on me and the Audi. They have been waiting.

I buckle my lap belt. Draw it tight, straight back to my spine.

The light changes, and I turn left onto the approach to the ramp. Drive toward the freeway. Check my rearview mirror. The Mustang runs the red light and follows me. They're not trying to hide their interest. We all know what's going on here.

I retired six of their side. At the time, I was an unknown quantity. These two won't fuck around.

Accelerate to merge speed, pull into the eastbound traffic. The Mustang shadows me, two cars behind. I change lanes, overtake an eighteen-wheeler, hide in front of the big boy. The Mustang accelerates and takes up position on my left quarter.

Look over my left shoulder. Take in my pursuers with a

glance. Young guys. Late twenties. Leather jackets. Dark, curly hair and piercing eyes. The guy in the passenger seat unlimbers an Ingram M-10. Compact, but heavy. It's a steel box that fires from the open bolt. A compact submachine gun, .45-caliber, thirty-round magazine. Very high rate of fire —a thousand rounds per minute.

Not good. With that weapon, he can put a lot of rounds downrange in a brief firing window.

I surge away and dart in front of the Mustang. Firing through the windshield will be difficult for him. The plexiglass will deflect much of his first burst. They'll try to pull up beside me on the left for a clear shot through the passenger window.

The Audi can't outperform the Mustang straight up, but in this situation, it's no slouch. I put my weight on the gas and watch the needle run up to eighty miles an hour. I dodge around cars and vans. The Mustang races to keep up with me. The I-10 is three lanes each way with wide shoulders. Built for speed.

Doing ninety, I pass a ten-ton truck on its left side. The Mustang's snout fills my rearview mirror. The driver pulls onto my left quarter. The gunman sticks the muzzle of the Ingram out his window and opens fire. The bullets spit from the muzzle and my left rear passenger window shatters. I turn the wheel to my left.

The left side of my Audi crashes into the right front quarter of the Mustang and pushes it out of its lane. There's a van on the inside left lane, and the Mustang is bounced between us. The van's driver leans on his horn. The Mustang's driver struggles to keep control. I floor the gas and leap ahead. The needle swings to ninety-five miles an hour.

Fishtailing, the Mustang comes back under control, and

the driver tears after me. I weave among the cars, making it difficult for him to anticipate my next move. I make my way to the inside lane. He has to get on my left to give his gunner a clear shot. With me on the inside lane, he needs to drive on the shoulder. There's a low concrete divider separating the shoulder from the westbound traffic.

I could edge onto the shoulder to block him, but I don't want to risk running my left and right tires on two different surfaces.

He decides to try it. Veers onto the shoulder, gasses up to catch me. The gunner leans halfway out his window and cuts loose with the Ingram as I twist my wheel and put the Mustang into the divider.

The last fifteen rounds in the Ingram's magazine blow out my rear window. There's an unholy screech as my left quarter locks with the Mustang's right. The whole of the Mustang's left side scrapes the divider for thirty yards. A shower of sparks and a cloud of dust erupts from between the car and the concrete.

I floor the gas and surge ahead.

The driver of the Mustang has trouble getting his car under control. He drifts partway from the shoulder and back onto the highway. Loses control again as his drive wheel bounces onto a different surface. Horns blare as traffic swerves to avoid him. An eighteen-wheeler jackknifes. Its trailer swings across the freeway and rolls. The wreck blocks all three eastbound lanes, and cars pile up onto it from behind.

Check my rearview mirror. The Mustang's driver recovers and bears down on me. The gunner in the passenger seat drops his mag and reloads. The I-10 is making a wide sweep to the south and New Orleans. I cross traffic and make for the outermost right lane. I'll take the next off-ramp and continue the chase on city streets.

The interstate is elevated, and so is the off-ramp. The ramp slopes downward to ground level in a tight arc. Traffic signs warn drivers to reduce speed.

The Mustang rams my rear bumper. Not sure what that accomplishes. The gunner fires through his windshield. The Ingram's first .45-caliber rounds deflect as they pass through. The last few rounds make it into my Audi. One of them smacks into my front windshield from behind. I ease off the gas to take the exit ramp.

A throaty roar, and the Mustang accelerates as it swings to my left. The gunner hangs out his window. My eyes flick toward the ugly bore of the Ingram. No concrete divider here. I twist the wheel and put the Mustang into the guardrail. Sparks fly and metal screams. The Audi bounces off the Mustang for a split second, and I turn hard left again. Shove him through the rail.

The Mustang crushes the guardrail and goes airborne. Foot off the gas, I fight for control. My forearms burn as I grip the wheel at ten and two, hold the sweeping arc of the exit. From the corner of my eye, I see the Mustang launched from the ramp at sixty miles an hour. It plunges to earth, and there's a dull crash as it impacts from a height of fifty feet.

I come off the ramp and find myself driving on ordinary city streets. I don't see a fireball in the rearview mirror. Lucky the wreck didn't explode. There's going to be a crushed lump of torn metal, broken glass and smashed plastic. All of it mixed with shattered bone and lacerated human flesh. Blood will mix with leaking gasoline and coolant.

Clouds of dust and smoke rise from the I-10 highway. A helicopter circles the pileup. I can't tell if it's a police or news helo. Whichever it is, their attention is focused on the traffic jam, not the source of the chaos. It'll be hours before they get an idea what caused the disaster.

The exit ramp delivered me to a quiet street. I park the car, unbuckle my lap belt, and get out. Jog past the ramp and the concrete supports. Look around for witnesses. There are none. The area under the raised highway and ramp is isolated. The world's attention is focused on the freeway.

Gasoline fumes hang in the air. There, beneath the ramp, the crushed Mustang sits upright on its four wheels. It landed on its nose before falling back. The engine has been crushed into the driver's compartment. I circle the car once, sniffing gasoline, looking for any sign of fire. There is none.

There's a gaping hole in the windshield on the passenger's side. The head and torso of the gunner is sticking out of the hole. He's lying face down on the bent hood. The crown of his head and the top of his face have been pulped. The plexiglass has been splashed with blood. His arms are flat to his sides, and his hands are still inside the car.

I grab him by the shoulders of his leather jacket and pull his body out onto the hood. Reach into his hip pocket and remove his wallet. Step to the passenger door. The frame has been jammed against it. There's no getting that sucker open.

The passenger window's been rolled down to allow him to shoot. How convenient. I stick my head and one arm into the car. A bunch of spent brass is scattered across the floor. I recover the Ingram and a canvas sack of spare magazines. Sling the sack over my shoulder and across my chest, check the Ingram. Very compact weapon, but incredibly *dense*. It's a heavy bitch, heavier than an M16 rifle, almost as heavy as a Thompson submachine gun.

Bolt forward, the weapon's empty. I drop the magazine,

open the bolt, check the chamber and bolt face. Walk around to the other side of the car.

The driver has been crushed behind the wheel. His face is unmarked, but his belly and chest are smashed. Blood has exploded from his mouth and nose. He's wearing a crimson bib. I twist my fingers in his hair and pull him back from the wheel. I can't reach his wallet. Lift his shirt tail and pull a SIG P226 with a fifteen-round mag from his waistband. Can't find any spares. I check the weapon and stick it under my shirt.

I turn away from the car. I'm tempted to light it up, but decide against it. The crash has escaped attention so far, no need to advertise. I walk back to the Audi. Stick the Ingram into the canvas sack with the ammo, set it on the passenger seat. Start the car, put some distance between myself and the ramp.

Somehow, I've been delivered to a large cemetery. The Audi is surrounded on either side by endless gardens of stone. How appropriate. I switch on the Audi's radio. It's a local station, maybe I can catch some news. A soft, jazzy song issues from the speakers.

To conceal the Audi, I park next to a big stone mausoleum. The structure is taller than the car, with a peaked roof supported by Doric columns. It's a facsimile of the Parthenon. I leave the engine running, the radio on. Get out and do a turn around the vehicle. It's not too bad. Rear window and left rear passenger window blown out. One starred bullet hole in the middle of the windshield. Some bullet holes in the trunk.

The whole left side is badly dented and scraped, but that could have happened anytime, anywhere. I won't draw *too* much attention.

Hertz is insured.

I take a deep breath and look around at the crypts. New Orleans is at or below sea level, which makes for a high water table. Bodies buried underground have a macabre tendency to float into people's backyards after storms.

Ninety percent of burials in New Orleans are above ground. In many cemeteries, bodies are kept above ground in tombs, where they completely decompose in hot, humid weather. By law, a tomb cannot be opened for a year and a day, to allow one full summer to completely decompose the body. The tombs are not airtight, to allow gasses to pass freely, facilitating decomposition.

After sufficient time has passed, the remains are removed and placed in memorial urns or otherwise packaged for the families. The crypt can then be reused. This practice amounts to cremation without cremation.

New Orleans. A haunted city of peculiar rituals surrounding death. What did Shakespeare write? "The evil that men do lives after them, the good is oft interred with their bones."

I get back in the car and swing the door shut. Drive away from the scene of the crash, try to find Pontchartrain Boulevard. Make my way to Storyville.

Time to meet Ellie.

10

DAY TWO - STORYVILLE, 1600 HRS

I drive into a parking lot around the corner from the *Gazette* office on Basin Street. Pick a space far away from other parked cars. Lean back in my seat, draw my phone from my pocket. First thing, I look for a restaurant and make a dinner reservation. My second call is to Stein.

"Breed," Stein says.

"Hi. Do you want to go first?"

"Sure. Still nothing on Victoria Calthorpe. I'm having the FBI visit her previous employer and ask questions formally. We hit pay dirt on Mark Luka, though. He's Albanian Mafia. Never been arrested, but the FBI and NOPD have files on him as thick as phone books."

"I can smell bad news."

"He runs human trafficking out of Kosovo, Bosnia, Croatia, all of Eastern Europe and former Yugoslavia. His latest action is cheap Ukrainian product that he ships to the US via Mexico and the Gulf Coast. He has a reputation for extreme brutality."

"Just women?" I ask.

"As far as we know."

"How big is his operation?"

"There are bigger operations, but he's expanding. He's engaged in turf wars, but his territory is secure for the moment." Stein pauses like she's checking notes. "He started by trafficking in Europe, then branched into the United States. The US operation started small but picked up in the last three years. He needed an outlet for the Ukrainians. Fifty percent of the prostitutes in Europe are Ukrainian refugees. It's supply and demand—as more of them flee west, they depress prices."

"Hate it when that happens."

"So did Luka. By shipping women here, he firmed up prices in Europe and found a rich new market. There was also less competition from locals, who tend to supply Latin American product."

"What's he doing buying hospitals?" I ask.

"Luka is doing very well for himself," Stein says. "He needs to launder money, so he's been investing in real estate. He owns properties everywhere in Europe, Britain and the United States. He owns property development companies, property management companies. I checked into Resurrection General, and the story you heard is accurate. The parish got into trouble and he bailed them out. I understand he paid a fair price."

"That sounds odd."

"He's become a respected pillar of the community. It looks like he wants New Orleans to be his home base in America. Makes sense because of its southern exposure. He bought swampland on the west side of Lake Pontchartrain. Land the government couldn't give away. He built an artificial island."

"I heard he built a house on the lake."

"That's right. He used the same technology the Chinese use to build artificial islands. Katrina packed down all the mud and clay. He layered on more, then capped it with concrete. Raised to avoid flooding."

"Then he built a house on the island."

"It's a castle. You can see it from I-10. Luka's Island is on the Lake Pontchartrain side of I-55."

"West of Resurrection."

"Yes. On the other side of I-55 is Lake Maurepas."

I'm not sure where the geography fits in. "A lot of things don't make sense."

"Your turn."

"He's not trafficking the missing and murdered girls. And Bailey Mitchell doesn't fit at all."

"True."

"He has an army. Two of his hitters just tried to take me out."

"What happened?"

"They waited for me to get back from the swamp. Staked out the junction between Bayou Road, the I-10, and Resurrection. Tried to light me up on the I-10 highway. I killed them, but we caused a massive pileup."

"Wonderful. Have they made the news?"

"Not yet, but they will. They went off the ramp and crashed underneath the freeway." I open the hitter's wallet and read his name and driver's license number to Stein.

"I'll check him out," Stein says, "but I doubt we'll turn up anything remarkable."

"No, these guys were expendable. But whatever is going on, Luka wants me out of the way."

"How did they know to wait for you there?"

"Not sure. I don't think they followed me from Storyville. Two victims were found in that swamp. It's more likely that Luka had them stake out the Bayou Road, and I drove into it."

"That means you're getting close."

"I'm getting confused. I told you about the Voodoo angle. Taylor Purdy's murder site fits the pattern. It's older than Bailey's. No cat heads, no decapitated chickens. But these were both ritual murders. Mark Luka's not the type to get involved in human sacrifice."

"He could be sending a message."

"I don't think so, Stein. Luka's the kind of guy to cut up a girl's face, pour drain opener down her throat, or go to work with a soldering iron. The cleanest thing he might do is put a bullet in her head."

"That's a fair point."

"Was there anything of interest in the files Ellie copied?"

"No. I had a couple of our doctors look through them. Both Bailey and Rowan are perfectly healthy kids. They did say the records and tests were extremely detailed, far beyond anything that would be required for a routine physical. Otherwise, no surprises."

"I have to go, Stein. If you think of anything, let me know."

"Where are you off to?"

"I'm taking Ellie to dinner."

I FIND Ellie at the *Gazette* archive. She notices the canvas bag slung over my shoulder. The bag I was not about to leave in a car with its rear window shot out.

"Have you been shopping?" Ellie asks.

"You could say that."

The paper is closing up, and the receptionist has gone for the day. We stick our heads into Garnier's cramped office and thank him. He's preoccupied with writing a piece.

"If you find anything that looks like a good follow-up story, let me know."

"Count on it," I say. Already, I can tell the follow-up story will win the writer a Pulitzer, but we are nowhere near completing the picture.

I lead Ellie to the Audi. The first thing she notices is the bullet hole in the center of the windshield. The spiderweb of cracks.

"What happened?"

"I went to look at the swamp where Taylor Purdy was found. On the way out, I ran into two more bad guys, who tried to kill me."

Ellie does a turn around the car. The shot-out rear window isn't too bad. The destruction was total. From a distance of twenty feet, it's hard to tell the glass is missing. The scraped left side is another matter. The dents are horrible, and the hubcaps are gone. It looks like there's more silver paint from the Mustang than blue from the Audi.

We get in the car, and I set my canvas sack on the floor on the passenger's side. Ellie has to stretch her legs over it. "What *is* that?"

"A machine gun."

"Cool! Where did you get it? No... I can guess."

Yesterday, as Ellie and I fled the Ruby Slipper, I noticed a parkade on Iberville. It's right around the corner from the Palace Café. I drive to it and find a spot on the third floor away from other cars.

Again, I'm struck by how much better New Orleans looks at night. The dinginess of the streets disappears in the glitz of the lighted clubs, bars and restaurants. Canal Street is the boundary between the French Quarter and the Warehouse District. The Palace Café is on the northeast side of Canal—the French Quarter side.

From across the street, the Palace doesn't look like much. There's a big sign on the roof announcing its presence to the world. The building itself is flanked by a sunglasses shop on the left and a liquor store on the right. The next block over is a Marriott hotel.

The Palace is a four-story building. You can look through a big window into the kitchen to watch the chefs at work. The first floor is a regular café with Formica tables and a bar. Ceiling fans turn lazily. Dress is casual. I lead Ellie inside, and we're guided up a spiral staircase.

The second floor is nice. It's a high, circular mezzanine that allows you to look down onto the first floor. The tables are set with white tablecloths, china and silverware. The lighting is warm, with an amber cast. I order a beer. I'm glad Ellie orders a Coke. I know she's got ID, and Stein's IDs will stand up to rigorous scrutiny, but I like to think of Ellie as a wholesome kid sister.

We set our haversacks on the floor between our legs and the rail. Ellie's bag never leaves her side.

"We can treat ourselves to some New Orleans food," I tell her. "I'm going to have gumbo."

"Me too," she says. "But tell me what you found."

"Wait one." I signal the waiter and order for us. When he's gone, I turn back to Ellie. "The Taylor Purdy site was exactly like the Bailey Mitchell site. I'm convinced someone was practicing Voodoo there. I think these were ritual killings."

"Human sacrifice," Ellie says.

"If you like, yes."

"I've been reading up on Voodoo. *Obeah*, which is New Orleans Voodoo. It's an ancient religion that gives practitioners power to make requests from the gods. There are strictly prescribed rituals that have to be followed to the letter. Some of the most powerful rituals involved human sacrifice. In particular, the sacrifice of children."

"Why children?"

"Children's spirits are the most pure and valuable."

Of course. There's a simple, almost common-sense logic underpinning the religion.

"Practitioners of *Obeah* have very intimate relationships with their gods," Ellie says. "The spells and ceremonies are precisely formulated. There's nothing random about it. Einstein said, 'God does not play dice with the universe.' That's what *Obeah* is all about. Predictable results. When they follow formal rituals, their gods possess them. The god enters a practitioner's body and interacts with followers directly. Makes demands of them, accepts or declines requests. There is one proviso... a supplicant cannot make a malefic request."

"What's that?"

"You can't make a request that hurts someone else."

Ellie never ceases to amaze me. Her ability to learn and synthesize is unsurpassed.

The last time I saw Albertine, she was walking with Bastien and Rémy toward the swamp. Carrying her yellow shopping bag. Now I'm wondering what was in the bag.

I focus my attention on Ellie. "Mark Luka, who owns the

hospital, is an Albanian gangster. He's into sex trafficking. His men tried to take you at the Ruby Slipper. Two more tried to kill me today. This all started when you were caught in Calthorpe's office. They don't know what you found, but you need to be silenced. I'm involved, so they want me too. That's all very clear. The problem is that it looks like Bailey and Taylor were kidnapped for Voodoo, not trafficking."

"Voodoo isn't Luka's business."

"No. It feels like there are two tracks going on here, and Rowan is involved in the Voodoo track."

The waiter sets a huge pot of steaming gumbo in the middle of the table. Gives us each a bowl, and ladles helpings for us. Ellie and I are famished and make short work of the meal.

I glance at my watch. There's another issue to deal with, and it bothers me.

"Ellie, there's one more thing."

"What's that?"

"There is no place in New Orleans that's safe for us. By now, Luka's people have found our hotel on Royal Street. He had the junction from I-10 to Resurrection staked out. He'll have both our hotels staked out. We caught them by surprise once because they didn't know what they were dealing with. Next time, we won't have that advantage."

"What are you saying, Breed?"

"I want you to go back to Pensacola. I'll deal with this. I'll find Rowan. I promise."

Ellie puts her spoon down and sits up straight in her chair. Glances around the Palace. Downstairs, a Cajun band with a fiddle, guitar, banjo and accordion have started playing zydeco music. One man is wearing a shiny washboard over his chest, strumming it with thimbles worn on his fingers. "Nice restaurant," she says. "Public place, so I won't make a scene."

"Ellie."

"Don't worry, Breed. I won't make a scene, but I'm not going anywhere."

"Be reasonable. These guys are not playing games."

"And you can't deal with them if you're dragging me along? That's easy to fix."

Ellie gets up and strides to the staircase.

"Shit." I take money from my pocket. Toss enough on the table to cover dinner. I shoulder the Ingram and its ammo, chase Ellie down the stairs. "Ellie, wait."

She shoves past the Cajun band and makes her way to the front door.

Ellie bursts onto the street and storms up Canal. I doubt she has any idea where she's going. I grab her by the arm. "Ellie!"

A young college jock grabs *me* by the arm. "Hey, let her go."

Everybody's a fucking hero. I lock the boy's wrist and force him to one knee. Reach into my sack, grip the Ingram, give him a glimpse. Shocked, the boy stares at the weapon. I push him onto his ass. "Take a walk, Batman."

Damn, I've lost sight of Ellie. My eyes search the sidewalk for her fast-striding figure. Did she cross the street or turn a corner? No, there she is, dodging between tourists and party animals. No destination in mind. She's incandescent, walking off her anger.

I catch up to Ellie at the end of the next block. Grab and pull her onto Royal Street. Push her up against the side of a dingy coffee shop and pin her shoulders. Wide-eyed, she stares at me.

"Listen, Ellie. These guys are trying to kill us."

Ellie's eyes flood with tears. "When have people *not* been trying to kill us?"

I think of what her father did to Ellie and Rowan. The things she had to face alone on the streets of New York. However she's coped with abuse, however competent she's become, emotionally she's still a child.

She said "*us*." She thinks we're alike. The difference is, I *chose* my life. But when I chose, I didn't understand what kind of man I would become. A man who thinks of how to kill every person he meets.

"Ellie, I promise I'll find Rowan. But I can't find her and protect *you*."

Tears are pouring down the girl's face. Dribbling from her chin. She sniffles. "I can take care of myself."

"*Please*, Ellie. Don't make me worry about you."

Ellie plants her forehead on my chest. Clutches me and sobs.

11

DAY THREE - RESURRECTION BAYOU, 0000 HRS

Ellie's on her way to Pensacola, and I'm about to crash an *Obeah* ceremony. Albertine and the boys were up to something this afternoon. I think they were getting ready to party on the beach. All well and good, except the party might involve Rowan. The problem is, I didn't sense criminal vibes from any of them. Nothing more than petty crime, at any rate. But so long as Rowan is missing, I have to check everything out.

I park the Audi inside the tree line, a quarter of a mile from the housing project and the swamp. Shoulder my haversack and start walking. The night is black, and the squat, ugly buildings are dark against the starlight. The trees separating the buildings from the swamp are black.

There are thirty yards of clearing on my right. Shades of darkness stretch north from the road. The earth, the swamp, the lake, and the night sky. The sky is a beautiful midnight blue.

Closer to the project, I hear the muffled rattle of African

drums. Tom-toms. A soft murmur coming from the other side of the trees. I walk to the side of the nearest building and scan the ground. The buildings are dark. Only one or two apartments in the second row of buildings show dim lights burning in their windows.

I stride to the tree line. Ropes of Spanish moss slap me in the face, and I brush them aside. The beat of the drums grows more energetic, and I can hear rhythmic chanting. Through the foliage, I see the flicker of flames from a large bonfire.

Swallow hard. I reach into the haversack and brush the steel of the Ingram. Right now, my deepest fear is that Rowan is on the other side of the tree line. A human sacrifice waiting to be disemboweled. Offered to the gods in some sick ritual. I sent Ellie away because she was in danger. But I also sent her away because I didn't want her to see Rowan killed.

I crouch low and advance through the brush. The firelight grows brighter, and I smell the sharp sting of wood smoke. Two dozen people have gathered around the fire. Tall white candles burn on plates arranged in a seven-pointed star.

A dark girl, wearing a diaphanous white shift, dances around the fire. She's hopping from one bare foot to another, slender legs bent at ankle and knee. She moves in time to the rhythmic beating of the drums, sprinkling white flour on the earth. She makes one circuit, then dips her hands in a yellow shopping bag. Withdraws fistfuls of white powder, makes another circuit.

It's Albertine, and the shopping bag is the one she was carrying from the building this morning. The congregation chants and sways. They move to the beat of the drums and

Albertine's sensual dance. When she has finished tracing the circle, the drumbeats accelerate. She throws her face to the sky and bends her back like a bow. Spreads her bare legs wide and stamps her feet in the frenzied rhythm. Her flesh is soaked in sweat, and the filmy shift clings to her body, leaving nothing to the imagination.

Albertine's back is bent almost double. She thrusts her pelvis toward the sky in a frenetic parody of the sexual act. The damp shift clings to her, revealing a black triangle. A high-pitched keening sound issues from her lips, and her eyes roll back in their sockets. The congregation are clapping and keening in time.

Mouth dry, I find myself aroused.

One of the men in the congregation steps forward from the circle. It's Bastien, the Red Beard. He carries a basket to Albertine and sets it between her feet. Opens the basket and steps back, eyes riveted by her carnality. Albertine reaches forward and lifts a rooster and a razor-sharp knife from the basket. She holds the rooster by its legs in her left hand, the knife in her right. Continues her dance around the fire, offering the animal to each of the congregation in turn. Chanting, they reach for the rooster and touch it, rub themselves against it.

Albertine reaches up with the blade and slashes the bird's throat. A jet of blood spurts from the animal. The blood sprays Albertine's throat and breasts. Her whole body quivers from her head and shoulders to the tips of her toes. The orgasm seems to go on forever as the bird beats its wings against her breasts. As the animal dies, Albertine comes to her senses. She lays the bird on the ground next to the fire and steps back.

The congregation come forward, starting with those

closest to the bird. They touch the dead animal, like supplicants touching a saint's statue. Leave offerings on the blood-soaked earth. Coins, beads, car keys, little bags of M&Ms. The most unlikely things one can imagine.

When the crowd has finished venerating the rooster, Albertine picks it up by the feet. The bird hangs, slack, from her hand. She raises it over her head and displays it to all. Then, with one swift motion, she throws the corpse into the fire.

The drumming stops, and the celebrants embrace each other in turn. Hand clasps and hugs. They say goodbye to Albertine, who has emerged from her trance. The drummers pick up their instruments and walk away with the drums under their arms or in sacks over their shoulders.

Albertine stands alone, staring after her flock. After some time, she snuffs out each of the seven candles between her thumb and forefinger. Collects them and the plates they stood on, puts them back in her yellow shopping bag. Then she picks it up and walks toward the trees.

My heart races—I'm afraid she'll walk right into me. I shrink back into the shadows, watch her walk into the woods a few yards away. She's following a trail back to the housing project.

I release my grip on the Ingram. Stand and allow myself to exhale. I was afraid Rowan would be here tonight. That I would find Albertine and Mark Luka's gang performing a human sacrifice.

The flames are hypnotic. I stare at the fire for a long time. Then I turn and walk into the trees.

I GIVE Albertine an hour before I enter her building. The main entrance isn't locked. I don't know her last name, but there is only one name among the top-floor mailboxes that has the letter *A* for a first initial.

Walk up the stairs, blood roaring in my ears. Just because Rowan wasn't at the ceremony doesn't mean Albertine isn't involved. But nothing makes sense. How often does Albertine hold these little parties? I remember her interaction with Bastien and Rémy this afternoon. They look up to her. She's some kind of high priestess.

The clock is ticking. The more time I allow to pass, the more likely Rowan will wash up dead.

I knock on Albertine's door. The fisheye viewer darkens as she checks to see who's there. She'll remember me from this afternoon. The question is, will she talk to me?

Albertine steps away from the door. I hold my breath, wait for it to open. Not a sound from the other side. The seconds stretch to a full minute, then the bolts roll back, and the door chain comes off with a rattle. Albertine swings the door open. Not a crack, but a couple of feet. She's just come out of the shower, washed the blood off her face. Tossed the stained shift into the laundry. She's wearing a pale terrycloth robe, belted at the waist. She's naked underneath.

"You didn't call," I say.

Albertine laughs. "Breed, it's only been a few hours."

"I couldn't wait." The scary thing is, I'm not lying.

"Get in here," she says. Closes the door behind me, bolts it. I set my haversack on the floor.

We're still feeling the chemistry from this afternoon. Amplified a thousand times by the ritual she just performed. She from performing it, me from watching her.

I take Albertine's hand and pull her close. She doesn't resist, folds herself into me. We kiss, and she throws her arms around my neck. I reach down, undo her belt, and the robe falls open. A sweet, sensual scent, like island coconut, engulfs us. I slide one hand between the robe and her breast. Rub my palm in a circular motion against her erect nipple. She moans into my mouth. I slide the robe off so it falls about her feet. Reach between her legs, find her hot and slippery.

Go with the flow.

I'VE LOST track of the number of times we've come. We lie together, exhausted, staring at the ceiling. I roll out of bed and walk naked to the window. Open the curtains and stare into the night.

My sniper's eye didn't fail me. The top floor of the first rank of buildings looks over the trees and onto the swamp. It has a view of a thin strip of dry land.

The fire has not burned out.

Albertine rolls over on one elbow. She knows what I'm looking at. Makes the connection to our conversation this afternoon.

"I did see something," she says.

"I know."

"They drove right up to the tree line. Took the girl's body from the trunk of the first car. Carried her to the swamp and set her on the ground. Then they built the fire and did things to her. Threw her pieces in. When they were finished, they tossed her into the swamp."

"Why didn't you say anything? The police must have interviewed everyone in these buildings."

"They did." Albertine looks miserable. "We use the swamp for *Obeah*. That fire... we had a ceremony tonight. I was afraid the police would think we had something to do with the girl's death."

"Of course they would. Albertine, I watched you tonight."

"And still you came?"

"I couldn't help myself. And no, I do *not* think you are involved."

"We practice *Obeah* for good. Eighty years ago, all the great practitioners of *Obeah* came together and agreed to outlaw human sacrifice. These murders are sick... Evil."

"Have you told me everything?"

"Yes. They got back in their cars and drove off."

"How many cars?"

"Two."

I step to the bed and lie beside her. Run my hand through her thick, wavy hair. Stroke her shoulder.

Albertine buries her face in her pillow. When she looks up, her face is anguished. "Breed, you *must* leave New Orleans."

"I can't. I have to find my friend's sister."

She caresses my face and pulls me close. "When I lead the ceremony, gods come into me. They show me things."

I remember the beating of the drums, the chanting. Albertine's frenetic dance, her shift plastered to the lines and curves of her body. The sweat trickling down her legs, the orgasmic shudder, her eyes rolling back in her head.

"What kind of things?"

"Death. If you stay, you'll be killed."

The dream comes to me. It's always the same.

The screaming won't stop.

High-pitched screams of agony and terror.

The village is in southern Afghanistan. There are mountains to the east, of course, but the high ground consists mainly of foothills. Not nearly as difficult to navigate as the mountainous country to the north. This is poppy country, where Afghanistan's major crop is grown. My Delta Force team stages out of KAF—Kandahar Airfield.

Two of our men were taken the other day. They're being held in the village, which is Taliban-controlled. My spotter and I have been ordered by Lieutenant Koenig to infil and locate the prisoners. Evaluate the chances of a rescue.

Tarback and I are both qualified snipers. We rotate responsibilities regularly. Today is my turn as shooter. Our rules of engagement forbid engaging unless we can do so with a reasonable probability of escape.

We all know the chances of rescue are slim. A rescue force can go in with armor, or it can go in by air. Probably by both. The Taliban will be waiting. In the worst case, the prisoners will be killed immediately, the rescue force will take heavy losses, and the death of civilians will be inevitable. More of our men might be taken prisoner.

Two of us went in. Me with an M24 sniper rifle, and my spotter with an M4 to provide security. We know what the consequences will be if we are caught. I intend to kill myself before I let that happen.

We climb a low hill eight hundred yards from the village. Build a firing position.

That's when we hear the screams.

"What the fuck are they doing?" Moe Tarback asks.

I say nothing. Set my M24 on its bipod, take out a beanbag and shove it under the toe of the rifle's butt. The M24 is a modified .308 Remington 700 with a heavy barrel. A classic hunting rifle, one of the most accurate sniper weapons available. My first rifle, when I was twelve years old, was a Remington 700.

Tarback lies behind his spotting scope and takes out his gear. Laser rangefinder, Kestrel anemometer, a notebook of firing solutions for the M24.

With the scope at 3x, I scan the village. We have a good angle and I can see the square clearly. The screams continue, spaced with pauses as though the torturers are drawing out the exercise.

"I can't tell where the screaming is coming from," I say.

We're prepared to displace if we can find a better firing position. This hill is good. I can't see elevated positions closer to the village. It's hard to imagine a better angle.

"Neither can I." Tarback squints through the spotter scope. He's positioned himself behind me and slightly to my right. He wants to have as clear a view as possible of my bullet trace.

There are villagers going about their chores in the streets. Taliban are mixed among them. Every man in Afghanistan has a rifle. Whether it's an AK-47 or an old Lee Enfield handed to him by his grandfather. Rifles are the soul of an Afghan.

"Horizontal range 786," Tarback says. He has taken a reading with the laser rangefinder and inclinometer. Double-checked with the spotter-scope reticle. The horizontal range to a target is the distance from the shooter if one measures flat to the earth. When firing from an elevated position, the line-of-sight range is always longer than the horizontal range. The horizontal range is the correct range to use in the firing solution.

The rifle is zeroed at four hundred yards. I move my hand to the elevation turret and dial in the adjustment.

From his position behind me, Tarback counts the click-stops and checks my work.

The wind is blowing dust from the streets.

How convenient.

"Wind ten, right to left, full value. Deflect seven-point-five."

"Roger that."

I make no adjustment to the turrets. I know the windage, and I will shift my crosshairs by the appropriate hold-off. Wind speed and direction change frequently. I can move faster by cuffing the adjustments rather than dialing them in.

Slaughterhouse screams.

We lie there for hours. The blood-curdling screams continue. Spaced out, carefully paced.

Screaming uses energy. A man can't sustain full-throated screams for more than a few minutes. If torturers continue their work without pausing, their victim becomes exhausted and ceases to function. Some nerves continue to conduct pain stimuli. Others are dulled. The torturer can't tell the difference because the victim can no longer make noise.

The Afghans know this. Their women are skilled in the art of torture. They use knives and hooks, they take their time. They make a little cut, hook the flap of skin and peel. Breathe their victim's screams. While the women work, the men watch or stand guard. In this case, there are a lot of armed Taliban in the village. They expect rescue to come from the air.

Tarback is shaken. "God almighty," he says. "How long will this go on?"

"They'll make it last for hours," I murmur.

The screams lower in pitch over the course of the day. The winding down of a life, like the running down of a clock.

"There," Tarback says.

"I see them."

Two women in burqas are dragging a man from one of the houses. A naked carcass of raw, bloody meat. The thing's mouth opens, the sound beyond description. I see white eyes, white teeth. Ragged skin, black with dried blood, peeled from red skeletal muscles, white ribs, and the pink-white abdominal wall. Translucent, enclosing dark, violet bowel. Afghans cheer.

I force vomit back down my throat. Blink sweat from my eyes.

Ropes are tied around the man's wrists. They used those ropes to bind him inside the house. Now they are using them to drag him into the square. Like a slug, his body leaves a trail of blood in the dust. Through the scope, I can see flies swarming over everything. Half a mile away, I can smell it.

A third woman drags a second carcass from the house. This man is silent. They did more than flay him. They sliced him open and used the hooks to drag his entrails from his belly while he was alive. Piled the violet mass of eels on his chest where he could see them.

"Jesus Christ," Tarback breathes. He keys his mike. "One-Five Actual from One-Five Bravo."

"Go ahead, One-Five Bravo." Koenig's voice.

"Two, repeat two POWs dragged into square. Their skin's been taken off."

"Say again, One-Five Bravo."

"You heard me." Tarback looks away from the nightmare. Forces himself to bring his eye back to the spotting scope.

Koenig makes his decision. "One-Five Bravo, do *not* engage."

I make mine. "Update firing solution."

"Wind ten, right to left, three-quarters," Tarback says. "Deflect six."

I do a mental calculation, shift my hold-off slightly. Take up the slack in the two-stage trigger.

Wonder if I'm making a mistake. I know what I would want if I were lying there, helpless and dying.

Koenig yells into the mike. "Breed, do *not* engage."

I reach the moment of my natural respiratory pause and break the shot.

The carcass jerks. The screaming stops. It's like the air goes preternaturally still.

A cry rises from the Taliban and the villagers. I cycle the bolt, chamber another round.

Koenig knows I won't stop. "Goddamn you, Breed."

Fire.

One of the women dragging the prisoners goes down. I hit her center mass and watch the burqa crumple like a hollow suit of clothes.

Cycle the bolt a third time.

Fire.

The second woman's head jerks. No blood. The explosion of her head is contained by her clothing.

My heart is beating no faster than it was when I started

shooting. My breathing is slow and regular. The horror will hit me later.

Men point at our position. At eight hundred yards, we must look like specks.

"One-Five Actual," Tarback calls, "request immediate exfil. We are moving to LZ now."

Fire.

Miss. The third woman runs.

Cycle.

Fire.

The round catches the woman in the back, between her shoulders. She pitches forward and lies motionless.

I draw back the bolt. The magazine's empty. I fish in my pocket, take out a loose round, load the rifle manually.

Taliban are firing, running toward us.

"Let's go, Breed." Tarback packs the spotter scope.

To make sure the second man is dead, I take aim and put the last round into him. A cloud of flies explodes from the mass of shiny violet entrails heaped on his chest. That's when the horror overcomes me.

I WAKE UP, screaming. Always the same dream. It really happened, the action that ended my military career. I killed those men and women. Their blood is on my hands. It'll never wash off.

"Breed, what's wrong?" Albertine sits next to me in bed. One arm is around me, her hand gripping my shoulder. Her other hand is in mine. "Tell me."

"It was real. I killed them."

If she's shocked by the confession, she gives no sign. "It's over, Breed. It's past."

"Why do they keep coming back? They won't go away."

My eyes are wet. Can't believe I'm doing this.

Albertine lays her cheek against my shoulder. "This was not evil, Breed. This was *Legba*."

I allow myself to lie back in bed. Stare at the ceiling. "What is *Legba*?"

"Not what, Breed. *Legba* is a god. He reminds us of things we want to bury. If they remain buried, they rot and make us sick. Like a bad smell from an open grave. He comes in our sleep and brings them back in dreams so we will face them. He is called the trickster."

"How many of these gods do you have?"

"Seven," Albertine says, with exaggerated gravity. "You watched last night?"

"Yes."

"Then you saw the seven candles that I arranged around the fire. They are there in my sitting room. Ordinary candles, but when arranged around the fire, attended by a congregation, they are transformed. Each god is welcomed to our gathering. Each has his place so believers can pay homage and request favor."

Albertine props herself on one elbow and looks down at me. Lays her palm flat on my chest and strokes gently. "*Legba* comes to you when you sleep. That's why the dreams are always the same," she says. "You're not making them up. You're remembering them."

"How do I make them go away?"

"Tell me what happened."

"The women tortured our men. What they did was

unspeakable. I shot the men to hurry them along. I shot the women because they needed killing."

"You blame yourself."

"No, they needed killing."

"Would you do it again?"

"One hundred percent."

"You say that, but you don't believe it. To make the dreams go away, you must believe it."

"How do I do that?"

Albertine kisses me. "You've already started."

12

DAY THREE - LAKE PONTCHARTRAIN, 0900 HRS

The Resurrection Parish sheriff's department occupies a low, single-story bungalow at the southwestern end of town. The building is surrounded by a neat lawn, a concrete drive, and two parking lots. The front parking lot is small, with spaces for four cars. The rear parking lot is twice the size, space for eight. There are two police cruisers parked in front and three personal vehicles parked in the back.

I park the Audi in the rear lot, far from the personal vehicles. Get out, lock the Ingram and its ammo in the trunk. Somehow, I doubt anybody will steal out of a car parked behind the sheriff's office.

The receptionist is a pleasant woman in her thirties. "Can I help you?"

"I'm here to see Sheriff Kennedy."

"Is she expecting you?"

"No, but she knows me. I won't take much of her time."

The receptionist announces me, and Kennedy sticks her

head out of her office. "Breed. Didn't expect to see you so soon. Come on in."

Kennedy's office is simple, clean and bright. Eggshell white walls with framed photographs. Artistic photographs of the swamp. Tranquil, slow-moving waters, shaded by a canopy of trees and Spanish moss drooping to the surface. Photos of the lake at sunrise, with flocks of Canada geese silhouetted against a great orange orb.

"Make yourself comfortable, Breed." Kennedy throws herself into a leather recliner. "Day hasn't started to roll yet."

I sit in an armchair across from the sheriff and stretch my legs. "I came to see if you'd had any luck with the autopsy reports."

"Breed, it hasn't been twenty-four hours."

I choke down my annoyance. Kennedy doesn't seem at all bothered that there's a missing girl out there. That at least two other teenagers in similar circumstances have been murdered.

"Isn't it just a matter of Nurse Shelly emailing you the files?"

"Sure. Once she has sign-off. The hospital has procedures to follow before releasing confidential information. Even to law enforcement."

"What have you learned about Carmen Esposito?"

"You were right about her," Kennedy says. She slides open a desk drawer and reaches inside for a paper file. Hands it to me. "She was hit by a car on the Old US 51."

I accept the file and flip it open. It's a police report, not the girl's medical records or autopsy report. "Did you requisition her files from the hospital?"

"Yes. They'll send us all three."

Carmen Esposito's photograph is the same as the one Ellie showed me at the *Gazette*. The police report is a standard form, with details filled in by the deputy at the scene. The signature at the bottom is not Kennedy's. This incident was, after all, three years ago. I don't know how long Kennedy has been in her position.

The report includes a hand-drawn sketch of the scene. Old US 51 is a narrow, two-lane highway with woods and a shoulder on either side. It lies east of and parallel to the new, elevated I-55, the latter built because Old US 51 was submerged by flooding one time too many. A note informs the reader that there is swamp directly to the east. There's an X on the western shoulder labeled *impact*. Sixty feet north is a crudely drawn stick figure. The figure is lying on the southbound side of the road.

The girl's body was found shortly after dawn. It's annoying that the time of death is not listed—it'll be on the autopsy report. There are no photographs of the highway or surrounding woods.

"No photos?"

"That's all I found in the file," Kennedy says. "This happened before I became sheriff. I don't know where they are, or if they even took photographs."

"What do you think?"

Kennedy shrugs. "She was dressed in street clothes, so she wasn't out jogging. Looks like she was hitchhiking north. It was a dark night. That highway's not lit. It's easy for someone speeding to overdrive his headlights."

I want to break things.

Show her the sketch. "She was hit on the southbound shoulder. The impact flung her body, or she was dragged by the car. I don't know which."

Kennedy lifts an eyebrow.

"The body," I tell her, "landed north of the impact point, on the southbound lane."

"From which you conclude...?"

"Carmen Esposito was hit by a car traveling north. Whoever hit her was driving on the northbound lane, and she was walking on the southbound shoulder. Facing the oncoming traffic. That's where you *should* be if you're walking or jogging on a shoulder. Walk or run *facing* the oncoming traffic. The killer crossed the center line and hit her from behind. She saw his lights and ignored him—she felt safe. This was murder, pure and simple."

"The driver might have been drunk."

"I don't think so."

For a long time, we're silent together.

"I'm going to take a look at the scene." I check the police report and note the location of the incident—two miles north of I-10.

I close the file and push it across the desk to Kennedy. She straightens in her chair. "I'll take you. Wait for me out front."

The sheriff reaches for her phone and instructs a deputy to cover the town in her absence. I walk out to the front parking lot. There's no question in my mind Esposito's death was murder. The incompetence of the sheriff's department is infuriating. Never mind the accident occurred before Kennedy became sheriff. The investigation was shoddy work. Filing it as a hit-and-run was disingenuous.

Kennedy emerges from the building and allows the door to swing shut behind her. She unlocks her cruiser and motions me to the front passenger seat.

"It's not far," she says. "We'll be there in ten or fifteen minutes."

She pulls out of the parking lot, drives up the main street, and takes the I-10 westbound on-ramp. A smooth merge, and we coast on the freeway at a comfortable sixty miles an hour. To my right, the blue waters of the lake stretch to the horizon. It's not an attractive blue. The sky above is hazy with thin wisps of cloud, and the water picks up a bit of an algae cast.

I'm conscious that we've left Resurrection Bayou behind on the left.

Albertine is still on my mind. I'm sure she and her flock aren't involved. Her story about the killers dumping Taylor Purdy's body and burning its organs rings true.

What of her warning? She was completely sincere. Another time, I might have dismissed it as superstition, but I saw her dance. It was easy to believe she was possessed by gods. Ellie had told me that sort of possession was an element of *Obeah*.

Stein likes to say I'm unkillable, but it's only a matter of time before I'm retired by someone better, luckier, or nastier than I am.

What do they say about Voodoo? Spells kill people who believe. Spells become self-fulfilling prophecies.

I curse myself for being silly. Albertine didn't cast a spell on me. She warned me.

My reverie is interrupted by the sight of a great house rising out of the lake. I remember seeing only two comparable structures. One is Mont Saint-Michel, an abbey built on a tidal island in Normandy. It's half a mile offshore at high tide, accessible from the mainland at low tide. The second structure is St. Michael's Mount, in Cornwall, in

England. It's a castle and chapel built on a tidal island near Penzance.

The house I'm looking at is much smaller than either, but it's a mansion, nonetheless. Three times the size of the big houses in the Garden District, French colonial in style, with Greek Revival features. Two tall stories plus an attic floor. On either side are symmetrical wings. The wings are two stories, joined to the main structure. The island it's built on looks like a flat concrete pedestal rising out of Lake Pontchartrain. High enough to prevent the house from flooding, the pedestal has been covered with rocks and earth to give it a more natural appearance.

Lake Pontchartrain is a tidal estuary, but I don't think it sees much tidal activity. The artificial island has been built two hundred yards from shore. A slatted wooden bridge extends over the tidal marsh and connects it to dry land. There are boathouses and piers on both the shore and the landward side of the island.

Behind the big house, I see part of a second structure. A carriage house without the carriages. It occurs to me that Luka took the plans of a Louisiana plantation house and built it on his island.

"That's Mark Luka's house," Kennedy says. "We call the place Luka's Island."

In the Garden District, the Luka house would be magnificent. Surrounded by centuries-old oak trees and lush greenery, it would be beautiful. Out there, on the lake, something's missing. It's like the bones of a great house without its soul.

"I wonder if he can plant some trees on that island."

"It's a work in progress. I'm sure it'll look different a year from now, and a year after."

The anemic blue of the lake gives way to a green swamp.

To my right stretches a broad spread of treetops. Bald cypress, with tangled roots planted in swamp water. I-10 is elevated, but low enough so the treetops are at the level of the freeway.

A highway sign tells us to drive ahead for I-55 and turn off for Leblanc. Kennedy signals right and takes the Leblanc off-ramp. At ground level, she makes a few deft turns and drives north on an endless stretch of highway.

"This is Old US 51," Kennedy says.

I was right. The deputy's sketch on the police report doesn't do justice to the ground. Old US 51 is perfectly straight, and it stretches to the vanishing point. It's narrower than I thought it would be. Two narrow lanes, two shoulders, bald cypress trees on either side. It's built low on a swamp. The shoulder on the right is separated from the tree line by a canal of still water coated with a film of bright green algae.

Kennedy checks her odometer. "Old US 51 looks like this the whole way. There are no landmarks where the girl got hit. All we have to go on is that it's two miles north of I-10."

"I reckon that's good enough," I say.

"It'll have to be."

I'm conscious there's no other traffic on the road. It's narrow enough that the girl *could* have been hit by a drunk driver. Someone weaving across the center line. I still think the possibility is remote. A drunk would have run off the road.

Kennedy pulls over and parks on the right shoulder. Leaves her light bar flashing and gets out of the car. "Let's stretch our legs, Breed. You can see there's nothing special out here."

I dismount and follow the sheriff onto the blacktop. She's right. This stretch of Old US 51 is as good as any other. My eyes search a hundred yards on either side, looking for skid marks. Assuming we're at the right place, there's no sign that a driver tried to stop or swerve. Of course, such marks might have been removed by the elements over the last three years.

"There were no skid marks," Kennedy says.

"That makes it worse," I tell her. "No skid marks means the driver didn't try to stop. Didn't do anything to avoid her."

I walk to the opposite shoulder. Make a scuff mark with my heel and pace off sixty feet. I doubt the girl's body would have been thrown that far. More likely, the initial impact threw her fifteen feet. Then she got hit by the car a second time and dragged the rest of the way before tearing loose.

"It must have been ugly." I stare at the road, calculating distances and angles.

"It was."

What an odd thing to say. I turn to look at the sheriff.

Kennedy has drawn her Glock 17 and is holding it on me. "Don't move, Breed. Keep your hands where I can see them."

I search that strong, attractive face. A woman who knows what she wants, and she's decided how to get it. Sold her authority to the highest bidder.

"You weren't the sheriff three years ago," I say.

"No, I was a deputy. Let's go back to the car. I doubt anyone will come by, but if they do, we don't want them to see this little scene."

Kennedy gestures with the muzzle of the Glock. We walk back to the police cruiser and stand on the shoulder between the cruiser and the tree line. It's swamp. Step off the shoulder and you're in shin-deep water.

"Who's paying you, Kennedy? As if I couldn't guess."

The sheriff pulls her phone from her pocket and hits a speed dial. "You know where to find us," she says. Disconnects the call and puts the phone away. The muzzle of the Glock doesn't waver.

Can I reach my own pistol before she pulls the trigger? Don't think so. I decide to wait for a better moment.

"You're pretty resilient, aren't you?" Kennedy smiles. "You took out our two men on the freeway. It took all night to clear up I-10 eastbound."

A gray Taurus sedan approaches from the south and pulls up behind us. The doors swing open and four men get out. They're plain-looking. Jeans and work pants. The driver's wearing a black Patagonia windbreaker. The guy from the right passenger seat is carrying a 12-gauge with a pistolized grip. Remington 870 pump with a fourteen-inch barrel. Four-round tubular magazine and one in the chamber, assuming he's ready for work. Big guy, work shirt, dark blue puffer vest. The two men in back wear black watch caps and work shirts. They're carrying Ingrams and haversacks of magazines slung across their chests and shoulders.

Kennedy holsters her Glock. "Leave him for the gators, boys."

I watch the sheriff get into her car, do a U-turn, and head back to town.

"You heard her," the driver says. "Into the swamp."

The man with the shotgun motions me to the tree line. I lead the way and step into the shin-deep ditch next to the road. The air smells of salt water, grass and algae. I wade to the tree line. The four men follow me in single file. Shotgun first, followed by the two Ingrams. The driver brings up the rear. Team leader. He's carrying a SIG in his waistband.

Into the trees, the water gets deeper. We're in it up to our knees, tripping on underwater roots. The swamp is beautiful. Tall cypress trees stand like ranks of silent sentries lined up on the shore. Festooned with Spanish moss, a thick green curtain. The water shines like polished glass, reflecting the images of the trees towering over the shoreline. The air is filled with the cheeps and high-pitched whistles of water thrush calling each other.

On patrol in the swamps, we used to cut slits in our pants legs and then sew up the seams. The slits allowed the water to flow in and out. Made it easier to move.

My skin crawls at the thought of pythons and alligators.

"That's far enough," the driver says. "Get it done."

The guy with the shotgun prods me in the back with its muzzle.

He's made the only mistake I need. He should have let me get well ahead. By prodding me, he tells me exactly where his weapon is. I turn sharply to my left and into him. Trap the shotgun under my left arm and drive the heel of my right hand straight up under his chin. Follow through, drive his head back with enough force to break his neck. I grip his throat, twist my hips, and throw him down over my right leg.

Take the shotgun, turn it on the first gunman on my left. Pull the trigger, watch the double-ought buckshot blow a group of pellets as wide as my fist into his sternum. He drops the Ingram and falls back into the turbid water. The splash sprays water high enough to make a glistening screen between me and the other two men. No time to pump the action—the man on the right is bringing up his Ingram. I swing the shotgun like a club across his forearm, knock the muzzle of the submachine gun down. He cries out as he pulls the trigger. There's a burst of gunfire, and the .45-caliber bullets send up a series of waterspouts. The driver thought everything was handled. He didn't bother to draw his handgun. Now he goes for it, and I turn and run into the trees.

It's hard to run in knee-deep water. My pants are soaked and clinging to me. I duck behind a cypress as the driver cuts loose. *Pop, pop, pop.* One of the rounds hits the tree. I pump the action, stick the muzzle of the shotgun around the tree and fire. The man with the Ingram cuts loose a long burst that empties his magazine in two seconds.

The driver thrusts his arms into the water. Retrieves the dead man's Ingram and ammunition.

I fire a third round in their general direction, turn and run. Two buzz saws rip the air. Both men are chasing me with the Ingrams. A bullet sings past my ear, splinters the trunk of a tree in front of me. The driver drops his mag and reloads.

Look around, try to orient myself. I broke to the right, more by instinct than anything else. I'm running in the direction of town, which is good. It's twenty miles to Ponchatoula in the other direction.

The guy in the watch cap fires a short burst, no more than two or three rounds. He knows that weapon sprays fifteen rounds a second, and he's trying to be economical with ammo. I dodge between the trees.

They're stalking me. One man moving left, the other right. The shotgun isn't ideal for this kind of combat. It's a powerful weapon at close range, but it's limited by its magazine. Right now, I'd give anything for an M4.

Old US 51 is to my right. Head in that direction, and I'll find dry land. In here, among the trees, I have cover and concealment.

I stop with my back to a tree. Look left. The driver will be approaching from the direction of the road. The man in the watch cap will approach from the woods. One from each side. Which will move first?

Turn to my right, stick the muzzle of the Remington around the cypress.

The driver sloshes through the swamp water. He dives for cover behind a tree. I fire, and the shotgun bucks in my hands. The blast of buckshot blows bark from the cypress, and he flattens himself against it. Makes himself very small.

The other guy sprints forward. It's a sensible tactic, a kind of bounding. One man draws my fire, then goes to ground while the other man charges. They work their way forward, closing the distance. The Ingrams afford them superior firepower, and they are using it to full advantage.

I pump the action, eject the spent shell casing. Damn. The gunman only had four rounds in the tube. I drop the Remington, reach under my shirt, and draw the SIG. The driver dashes forward and I squeeze a round off.

"Come on out, boy, and we'll make it quick," the driver yells.

The man in the watch cap sprints forward. I fire, and he dives behind another tree.

I can't play this game for long. Turn and run for another copse of trees. No game changer leaps to mind. Maybe if I get into a position where I can charge one of them, I'll be able to even the odds.

Fucking swamp. The cypress trees grow out of the swamp water, standing on roots that sprawl like wooden pedestals. Scattered around them are short, ugly stumps— cypress knees —literally knee-high. Many are blunt, but many are cones, eight inches across at the base, that taper to sharp points like stakes planted in the swamp. I trip on a root and fall face-first. Suck in a mouthful of salty water, struggle to my feet and spit it out.

Duck behind a large cypress. Its roots spread several feet across like a massive tripod. I drop low and sit perfectly still with my back propped against one of the trees. I'm up to my chest in brackish green water. Soaked and cold to the bone. Strain my ears to detect which of them will come first. It's a risk, but I'll let them get as close as I can before I make a move.

The driver fires, and the other man sprints. As quickly as a man can sprint in knee-deep water. I hold my fire.

"Are you giving up, boy?"

Guy's got a big mouth. He's giving his own position away. He's a lot closer to me than I thought. Maybe closer than he thinks.

I've broken the pattern and got them doubting themselves.

The Ingram chatters, and bark flies. I turn in the direction of the driver, who's broken cover. The trees still provide cover from the other man's submachine gun. Too late, I raise the SIG. I was right—the driver's on top of me as I fire. One round. I hit high on his chest toward the right shoulder. He crashes into me and drops his Ingram. Seizes my wrist with both hands and slams my gun against the tree trunk. Once, twice. The strength of desperation. I drop the SIG and it falls into the water with a splash.

We glare at each other, teeth bared. I tear free of his grasp. He punches me in the side, but has no strength. We grapple, and I seize his collar with my left hand, scoop his left leg from behind the knee. Lift him bodily into the air as he clutches my shoulder. I dump him onto one of the pointed cypress knees and drop on him with all my weight.

The sharp cone penetrates his back. His eyes snap wide and he screams in my face.

"Lou! Lou!" his buddy yells.

The guy in the watch cap is coming. I roll off the driver—he's impaled on the stake. His mouth works without sound. I thrust my hands into the swamp water, scrabble around on the bottom for my pistol or the Ingram. Can't find either.

Bullets kick up the water around me. I throw myself down. Crawl on hands and knees to the cover of the trees. The man unloads his Ingram, and bullets slap into the tree trunks as I duck behind them.

The man in the watch cap is rushing from cover, firing on the run. Short bursts, meant to keep me down as he closes the distance. I sit behind the trees, in chin-deep water. When he comes around, I'll try to close when he reloads. Take him hand-to-hand.

There's movement behind trees fifteen yards ahead. Shadowy figures move behind the cypress trunks. My stomach clenches and my breath freezes in my chest. A rifle barrel juts from behind the cypress, resting against the shoulder formed by the roots and trunk. The bore of that barrel looks as big as an artillery piece.

The gunshot sounds as loud as a cannon. A puff of smoke bursts from the muzzle. God almighty, is he firing black powder? The man running with the submachine gun is stopped in his tracks. A hole the size of a golf ball explodes in his chest. He drops the Ingram and pitches backward into the swamp, arms outflung.

Bastien emerges from cover and advances with a deliberate step. He's carrying a big-bore carbine. Thumbs the breech open and drops a spent shell casing. Loads another round and rolls the breech shut. He walks past me to the man floating face-up in the water. Takes careful aim and fires another elephant round into the man's face. The face pulps and collapses on itself. All smashed flesh and bone. The creature floating in the water is no longer human.

Rémy steps from behind another tree and advances. The bumpkin is carrying a Winchester 1892 lever-action carbine. I stare at him, then turn to Bastien.

"What are you doing here?" I ask.

Bastien grunts. "Albertine. She said you need help."

"How did she know where to send you?"

"Don't ask questions," Bastien says. "Gods talk to that girl."

Really.

I step to the dead man in the watch cap and jerk his SIG P226 from his waistband. Check its condition, stuff it in my own. Thrust my hands in the water and retrieve his Ingram, take his sack of magazines.

The driver remains impaled on the stake, spread-eagled. His arms and legs hang limp on either side, hands and feet submerged in greenish-brown water. He stares at the tree-tops while blood froths from his mouth. I raise the 226 and shoot him between the eyes.

Decock. Search the body and find two spare mags. Pocket those, stick the 226 in my waistband. Relieve the corpse of its sack of Ingram magazines. Sling it with the other one over my right shoulder. I rummage around in the corpse's pockets, retrieve his car keys and wallet.

"Let's go," Bastien says.

I raise my eyes to the Cajun. He and Rémy are standing with their rifles cradled in the crooks of their arms. They're waiting for me.

"Alright," I say. "Thanks for your help."

I'm fascinated by Bastien's weapon. It's a single-shot Remington rolling-block carbine. Probably a .43 Spanish. The kind popular in the late nineteenth century. They're inexpensive and readily available on the used market. A single-shot rifle imposes ammunition discipline on a shooter.

Black-powder ammunition. Bastien's rifle came into its own in the 1860s. It's a Civil War-era piece, and its soft lead ammo does far more damage than modern military ball. The .43 Spanish has an actual diameter of .439 inch. The .308 full-metal jacket weighs 147 grains. The .43 Spanish fields a hefty 383-grain cast-lead bullet.

Imagine a soft lead bullet more than twice as heavy as a modern military round. Those chunks of death expand on impact. One hit can amputate a limb or leave it dangling by a ragged strip of flesh. Center mass, the wound channels are devastating. For anyone who likes the idea of throwing a big piece of lead through a soft target, it packs a powerful punch.

How did he get it? Remington rolling blocks and similar weapons were widespread in the late nineteenth century. Countries that didn't have their own arms manufacturing industries bought them by the thousands in slightly different calibers. Use of the rifle was so widespread that the ammunition was widely manufactured. The brass for .43 Spanish is still manufactured today, but the shooter has to hand-load his ammo and cast his own bullets. You can load smokeless powder, but that's not what I saw Bastien shoot.

"Come with us," Bastien says. "Talk to Albertine."

That sounds like a good idea. Sheriff Kennedy is bound to call these men to make sure I'm dead.

Bastien and Rémy are men of few words. We walk to the road. Getting back on dry land isn't the relief I hoped for. I'm soaked and my clothes are clinging to me. The Cajuns parked their pickup behind the Taurus.

I climb into the Taurus, set the Ingram and sacks of magazines on the passenger seat. It seems the Ingram and SIG are standard weapons for the bunch I'm up against. I start the engine, put it in drive, and follow the Cajuns as they make a U-turn and head south.

Events are moving far too quickly for me. There are too many questions and not enough answers.

Do I really believe the gods told Albertine I was in trouble? Last night she warned me that if I stayed, I would die.

I cannot allow myself to believe this. But when I faced that Ingram bare-handed, I thought I was going to die.

My phone still works. I punch Stein's speed dial.

"Breed, where have you been?"

"Trying to stay alive. Sheriff Kennedy tried to have me killed."

"How did that happen?"

"Carmen Esposito was murdered three years ago. That hit-and-run was premeditated, and then-deputy Kennedy was involved somehow. The file on Esposito was criminally incomplete. I had Kennedy take me out to the crime scene—lonely highway at night. It was obvious the girl was deliberately run over. Kennedy pulled a gun on me. Had four of Luka's hitters come over and take me for a walk in the swamp."

"Do you know why they killed those kids?"

"No, that's the problem. Esposito was supposed to end up like Bailey Mitchell and Taylor Purdy, but something went wrong. They had to kill her without carving her up."

"We're no closer to finding Rowan. If Luka is behind this, two obvious possibilities are his house and the hospital."

"We don't dare guess wrong."

I'm lying on Albertine's bed while my clothes tumble in her dryer. I reach for a book lying on her nightstand. The cover is a pretty watercolor of nubile young girls playing by the seaside. The title of the book is in French: À l'ombre des jeunes filles en fleurs. One of Proust's works.

"You read Proust in French?" I ask.

Albertine stands naked by her window, looking out over the cypress swamp and the lake beyond. "Of course," she says. "I'm Cajun."

I flip through the well-thumbed book. Set it on the bedside table. "What's it say?"

"It says *In the shadow of young girls in flower*. In nineteenth century France, it was a not-too-veiled reference to young virgins having their first period."

"How old were you when you lost it?"

"What do you mean?"

"You know, *it*. Your *flower*."

Albertine laughs. "Breed, were you *born* without a filter?"

I shrug.

"Thirteen," Albertine says.

"Who was he?"

"I don't know. It was at a ceremony—*chevalier*—I was mounted by the gods."

I shake my head. "Gods have sex with you. Gods talk to you."

She turns to me with a wicked smile. "I sure heard them five minutes ago."

The girl's orgasms were staggering. I study the long lines

of her arms and legs, her small, upturned breasts. Her nipples are as hard and thick as oversized pencil erasers, the aureoles as wide as Kennedy halves. Her smooth flesh is shiny with sweat.

"Be serious. How did you know I was in trouble? How did you know where to send Bastien and Rémy?"

"Breed, there are evil forces out to destroy you. Those forces are working through an *obayifo*—'he who steals the children.' Very bad *Mayombe*. I practice *Obeah*, which is only for good. I told you gods come to me. In ceremonies and in my dreams. After you and I met, they told me to help you. I'm doing what I can, but the evil against you is very strong. *Mayombe* is evil Voodoo. I can't explain it better than that. At some point, you either believe, or you don't."

"This *obayifo*... is it a god or human?"

I can't believe I'm starting to take this stuff seriously.

"The *obayifo* communes with evil gods for personal gain."

"Is there a *Mayombe* cult in New Orleans?"

"It's not a cult, Breed. The best way to look at it is... as a church."

"A church."

"What do you call a place where a congregation communes with their gods?" Albertine shrugs. "The *obayifo* either practices alone or with others. Just as you and I are able to worship alone or with others."

"So this man might be working alone."

"The *obayifo* does not have to be a man."

Great. It's Mark Luka *or* Sheriff Kennedy. My head is starting to ache.

Albertine's not out to hurt me. I believe that much. But I can't accept this witchcraft.

"Are my clothes dry yet?"

"Another half hour," she says.

"Half an hour."

The girl licks her lips. "Can't you think of anything to do with half an hour?"

"I can't imagine."

Albertine runs to the bed and pounces on me. "Gator gonna eat you, baby!"

13

DAY THREE - RESURRECTION GENERAL, 1200 HRS

I stare at the wall in a consultation room at Resurrection General's emergency department. It wasn't hard to get in. I presented myself, feigned stomach pain and was triaged to the bottom of the list. A nurse showed me to the room and told me to wait my turn.

Perfect. I look around. I'm sitting in an armchair. There's an examination table with a black leatherette surface. A paper cover is disposable, meant to protect a patient from the previous patient's fluids. Or crabs. Or whatever. There's a set of cabinets. A blood pressure machine and cuff. A coat tree and a bunch of white lab coats.

I get up and pull one of the lab coats off the tree. Looks like it was cut for a girl. No way I'm getting into that. Put it back, take down another. Better, but the sleeves are too short and the chest won't close.

Third time lucky. Not bad. Maybe I should have gone to med school. There's no ID tag, just a couple of colored pens in the breast pocket. I check the ID card on the pocket of the other man's coat. No good, we don't look at all alike. I'll take my chances. If challenged, I'll just say I forgot it at home.

I step into the corridor, close the door behind me, and walk straight to the fire stairs.

There's a laminated plaque fixed to the wall. A floor plan of the hospital. I rip the plan off its double-sided adhesive strips. Step through the fire door and go down the stairs to the next floor, which has to be the first basement level. There are more stairs leading down, so there must be deeper levels.

What I want are the dead kids' autopsy reports. Presumably, I can get those off any one of the tablets conveniently scattered through the hospital. But if I can look at hard-copy files, I might see something that won't reveal itself on an 8½" by 11" screen. I'm sure I can find both in the pathology department. That's going to be in the basement. Near the morgue.

There are operating theaters on the second floor and the first basement level. The autopsy room is on the second basement level. Looks like a simple affair. I doubt Resurrection General's autopsy room sees much business. The histology lab is on the second floor. The morgue is across the hall from the autopsy room. Next to the morgue is a working office for the pathologists.

I descend one more flight to Basement 2. Push through the insulated fire door. It's equipped with a long, elbow-actuated handle. I step into a long corridor, the lowest level of the hospital. I consult the floor plan, go to the end of the hall. Walk past a pair of elevators. The air is cold, and my skin crawls. The walls are cement, covered with glossy yellow paint. I put my hand on the surface, withdraw it quickly. The surface is cold, smooth and clammy. Like something once alive, now not very.

The place seems deserted, and it's not hard to see why. It gives me the creeps.

I pass a wooden door on the right marked *Pathology Office*. Everything is quiet within. I turn the doorknob and peep inside.

The room looks like a regular corporate office. Brightly lit, modern desks. Cordless telephones charging in their cradles. Laptop computers set in docking stations with large flatscreen monitors. Each has a cordless desktop keyboard and mouse. There's a hospital tablet lying on one desk. I pick it up and fuss with it. Touch the screen, and it lights up. The cheesy Resurrection General wallpaper shows an attractive nurse and doctor bestowing their smiles on an affluent-looking boomer.

I decide to leave the tablet while I complete my exploration. Set it on the desk. To the right of the laptop is a huge, leather-bound anatomical tome. The pages are a foot wide and eighteen inches high. It has been opened to the section that displays the chest cavity. I notice that there are acetate pages beautifully illustrated in color. They have been arranged so that as one turns them, one successively peels back layers of the body. I lift each acetate page by one corner and turn it to reveal the underlying structures. First I peel back the skin, then lift off the breastplate of the sternum, then remove the numbered ribs. Finally, a nearly three-dimensional representation of the chest cavity is revealed. I lift out the lungs, and there it is...the heart, and the blood vessels that sprout from the muscular pump.

I force myself to look away from the reference. A gold ballpoint pen and a pad of drawing paper lie on the desk next to it. Someone has carefully reproduced the image of the heart sitting in the chest cavity. The reproduction has been drawn in meticulous detail. One might call it a labor of love. Notes have been carefully scrawled around it in a fine hand.

The drawing is incongruous in these surroundings. The laptop, monitor and tablet are of the twenty-first century. The drawing and notes appear to be from the eighteenth or nineteenth centuries. They were recently done, but look like they belong in the British Museum.

I pick up the gold pen. Engraved along the barrel in cursive script is the name of the owner: *Emile Durand*. Glance back at the drawing. That's what it looks like inside the good doctor's head.

Step back into the hall. There's another set of fire doors at the other end, and I walk in that direction. To my left are wide elevator doors. Twice as wide as the ones I passed earlier. This elevator is meant to carry gurneys loaded with passengers. Of course, they have to get bodies down here and back upstairs.

Fifteen feet down the corridor are two sets of butterfly doors, one either side. The first set on the left bears a sign that says *Autopsy*. The set on the right bears a sign that says *Morgue*.

Push through the doors into the autopsy room. It's big and plain. Four autopsy tables are set in a row. Unoccupied at the moment. Ranks of fluorescent lights extend the length of the ceiling. They have been spaced to provide even illumination. Each table has its own set of powerful lamps on wheeled stands. One at the head of the table, one at the foot. There's a tripod with a professional Nikon camera, ring flash, and medical lens.

On three sides are modular cabinets with sinks, hoses, racks of sample containers, and instruments. There's a refrigerator that I'm not keen to open. Everything in the room reminds the casual observer that the human body is ninety percent water. When it dies, when it's opened up, when it decomposes, everything around it gets wet.

The room reeks of formaldehyde. Not as bad as the stench of a battlefield, but strong enough to stay with you. I step to one of the low cabinets. There's a large sink on the left, a table to the right. On the table is a shiny stainless-steel pan. It's two and a half feet square and three inches deep. The bottom is surfaced with black tar.

What creeps me out is the dead cat lying in the pan. It's on its back, legs spread. Long pins have been driven through its paws and into the tar to hold it in place. Its head is thrown back, jaw slack. I'm glad I can't see its eyes. The animal's gray fur is matted with preservative. This is the source of the formaldehyde smell that permeates the autopsy room.

On the table to the left of the pan lies a surgical kit. The scissors and scalpel have been used. Bits of flesh cling to the scissors. The cat's abdomen has been carefully dissected. Opened up from pelvis to breastbone. The internal organs have been lifted out with care, irrigated to prevent them from drying out. They've been arranged in two columns, to the left and right of the cat's body.

The animal's right foreleg has also been dissected. An incision has been made the length of the long bones. The fur and skin have been parted with great care. The exercise has exposed the muscles.

Tablets of heavy drawing paper sit on the table to the right of the pan. There, two separate drawings have been made. One is a detailed illustration of the cat's viscera, with every organ identified and carefully labeled. The other drawing is of the musculature of the foreleg.

The illustrations look just like the reproduction of the anatomy reference in the pathology office. Artistic, with meticulous attention to detail. They look like something from the early nineteenth century. The notes and labels have been made in Emile Durand's hand.

This scene seems out of place. Resurrection General's autopsy room is for human subjects. Granted, it's a small hospital. The facility doesn't see much business, but this cat dissection is what I would expect to see at a college. Not at a working hospital.

These dissections have the appearance of a *hobby*.

I shiver. It's like Emile Durand doesn't have enough human beings to practice on, so he polishes his skills dissecting animals.

The smell of formaldehyde lingers in my nostrils. I turn and push through the butterfly doors. Can't leave the damn autopsy room fast enough. I cross the hall and open the doors to the morgue.

I find myself in an antechamber that constitutes the morgue office. There's a paper calendar on one wall. A wide kneehole desk bearing a desktop and a flatscreen monitor. There's a keyboard, mouse and mouse pad. Another of the ubiquitous tablets sits next to the keyboard.

The rest of the morgue office—all three walls—is occupied by steel filing cabinets. Those are the paper files I want.

I step through the interior set of doors and find myself in the morgue proper. Wall-to-wall banks of refrigerated steel coffins.

Shivering, I go back into the office and sit down at the desk. I pick up the tablet, tap it, and face the cheesy welcome screen. Another tap brings me to the login prompt. A blank field and a numeric keypad. Without hesitation, I type in 1-1-

5-9. The login page dissolves and is replaced by the desktop. The icons are exactly the same as the ones Shelly demonstrated to us.

Right on the first try.

People need to learn that using the same digit twice in succession makes their PIN materially less secure. It's a simple probability calculation, something snipers and artillery men get very good at when predicting the fall of shot.

I open up the folder labeled *Patient Records*. Locate Taylor Purdy. Her health reports and appendectomy are in one sub-folder. There's a separate sub-folder labeled *Autopsy Reports*. I locate her file and zip both her health report and autopsy report into one envelope. Attach it to an email.

The *From* field attracts my attention.

From: karen.shelly@resurrection.med

Use of any tablet is recorded and tracked. The tablet dies as soon as it leaves the hospital.

I email the files to myself and Stein. A warning flashes onto the screen:

Some recipients are outside your organization. Do you want to continue?

I hesitate. I'll chance it, but I'd rather send one email than three.

Carmen Esposito's health records and autopsy report are easy to find. I attach them to the same email. Finally, I locate Bailey Mitchell's autopsy report and attach it.

I take a breath, click *Send*.

Delete the zip files, delete the emails from the sent items folder. I have a feeling this business will be over long before Luka's cybersecurity does a full forensic exam. Then what will they find? Nurse Shelly sent files from the hospital to a black government email address. The lady will have some explaining to do.

Any security firm that enquires about Stein's email address will have the NSA crawling up their ass with a microscope. All their devices and software will be infected with keyloggers they can't even dream about. Then they'll find themselves visited by dapper young professionals wearing certain haircuts and expensive business suits.

I get up and go to the filing cabinets. There, I find Carmen Esposito. No health records. This place is just for autopsy reports. The last time a doctor will ever look at you. I carry the girl's folder back to the desk and open it.

Force myself to read the details. The girl's body was opened up by the impact. Getting dragged by the car over the road compounded the devastation. This wasn't the surgical evisceration performed on Bailey Mitchell and Taylor Purdy. This was a body caught on metal and ripped open. Bones crushed by a two-thousand-pound automobile traveling at sixty or seventy miles an hour and accelerating.

Cause of death: blunt force trauma to head and chest caused by automobile impact.

Attending pathologist: Dr. Emile Durand.

The photographs tell a grisly tale. As I look through the images, my outrage grows. Kennedy must have disappeared the photographs from the police report. This girl's parts must have been strewn over sixty feet of highway. I will have to sort out the sheriff before this is over.

My eyes scan a grisly full-length nude photograph of

Carmen Esposito shot from above the autopsy table. Her abdomen had been ripped open by the hit-and-run. Her flesh had been hooked on metal beneath the car. It had not been cut, but *torn* by the remorseless machine. The vehicle dragged her along the road while her contents spilled out. An arm and leg look broken, but were carefully aligned for the photo.

There—something catches my eye.

Easy to miss. The observer is so absorbed by the destruction wrought on the girl's body, he misses the discoloration around the girl's wrists.

And ankles.

Faint purple marks in this photo. Bilateral. Those are unlikely to have been caused by the impact.

I shuffle through the photographs. Pictures of the girl's wrists. Ugly purple ligature marks on dead gray skin. The same on her ankles. I saw those on torture victims in Afghanistan.

Under such circumstances, it was standard procedure to dissect the skin around the ligature marks. A good pathologist could determine things from the extent of subcutaneous bruising. Blood collection under the skin that does not show up on the surface. That tells the pathologist if the victim was tortured by binding. The Afghans like to flay their victims. Allied units like to use "stress positions" to minimize superficial indications of torture.

Durand did not dissect the girl's wrists and ankles.

A hit-and-run, there was no reason to suspect torture. But surely the ligature marks in and of themselves were suspicious.

I read the report again, line by line.

Durand did not mention the ligature marks in his report.

That was a gross omission. He forgot to destroy the photographs. Should have had Kennedy working with him.

Shake my head, check Taylor Purdy's photographs a second time. I start with the full-length photo. There are faint marks on her wrists and ankles that might have been ligatures. But they're so faint I can't swear to them. Easy to miss. No closeups of her wrists or ankles. No dissection. If they were photographed at all, Durand destroyed them.

I review Bailey Mitchell's photographs. No ligature marks.

Voices carry from the corridor. I shuffle the photos and reports back into their folders. Go to the cabinets and return the files. A man and woman are approaching from the direction of the elevators. I step to one side of the butterfly doors. If they enter, I'll dash past them, run to the nearest set of stairs and bail out.

The man and woman stop halfway down the corridor, and their voices fade. They've gone into the pathology office.

Time to leave. I sweep the morgue office with my eyes. Check to make certain I haven't forgotten anything. Then I step into the corridor and walk to the pathology office. The voices of the man and woman grow more distinct.

I recognize those voices. Nurse Shelly's warm tones, Dr. Durand's cold, precise diction. They are carrying on a conversation.

"—is not available for auction," Nurse Shelly says. "It has been sourced on special order, a four-point match. We have two kidneys and three lobes of liver available."

Shelly pauses. Listens to the other party on the phone.

"I'll say it again," she says, "the heart is not available. If you're not interested in the other items, there's no point continuing now."

Another pause. "Thank you," Shelly says. Then, "Cobra does not wish to continue."

"That is alright," Durand says. "The heart is time-sensitive; we must execute no earlier than nine o'clock tonight and no later than ten. The heart is only viable for six hours after death and has to be on that airplane on schedule. Whatever we get for the other items is a bonus."

"Imagine paying a hundred million dollars for a heart," Shelly says.

"It is *not* hard to imagine. One has to satisfy numerous criteria, one has to make it onto the list, one must wait one's turn. Wealthy men are not predisposed to wait their turn. Especially when their lives hang in the balance. Worse, rejection by the selection committee is a death sentence."

The sound of tapping on a desktop keyboard carries to the corridor. A pause, and Shelly says, "Python is prepared to bid ten million for the complete liver."

"Ah," Durand says. "I like it when the game becomes interesting. We have three lobes for sale. Each by itself is viable. The question—is the whole worth more than the sum of the parts?"

"Anaconda and Rattler are prepared to pay three and four each for a lobe."

"Excellent. We need an additional bid for three."

"I have a couple of potential players."

"Keep in mind," Durand says, "if the sum of the three does not exceed ten million, *all three* lose. At that point, they are *all* incentivized to raise their bids."

"I'll do what I can. In any case, we have a floor of ten million."

"Let us see how far we can run with this."

MIND REELING, I back away from the door and walk quickly to the fire stairs. Open the door, step through, and close it quietly behind me. Durand and Shelly were so casual in their discussion of the sale of stolen organs. It was as though they were not affected at all. Durand must be the surgeon. If a man can be *that* detached from butchery, surely he can destroy a body as thoroughly as Taylor Purdy and Bailey Mitchell were destroyed.

What kind of depraved gratification could he derive from performing such slaughter?

And Shelly. She must like to watch.

But... neither is the *obayifo*.

I climb two flights of stairs to the ground floor and return to the consultation room. Take off my lab coat and hang it on the coat tree.

Go back to the chair and sit down. I have what I came for, so screw it, I should just leave. They'll figure I got tired of waiting. I get to my feet.

There's a knock and the door opens. A young man in a lab coat pokes his head into the room. "I'm Dr. Spencer. Sorry to keep you waiting."

I smile. "It's alright, Doctor. I was just leaving."

"It's best I perform a quick examination."

"No, thank you. I'm feeling much better."

I excuse myself and step past the doctor. Five minutes later, I'm outside, walking to the parking lot.

Resurrection Parish is a bit hot with Sheriff Kennedy cruising around. By now, she knows I've killed four more of Luka's hitters. She's pulled my service record. Seen my qualifications, the deployments, the mysterious early discharge. Then a string of contract roles with carefully redacted descriptions. Many of them marked CLASSIFIED. She knows some kind of death machine is rolling around Resurrection Parish.

She won't know about Bastien and Rémy, and that's a good thing. Luka isn't short of resources, and I don't want him sending hitters after Albertine and her friends in Resurrection Bayou.

I drive east into Jefferson Parish and find a McDonald's. Order coffee and a blueberry muffin. Park the Taurus in an isolated corner. Pick up my phone and call Stein.

"I don't want to know how you got these." Stein is obviously looking at the files I emailed her.

"I stole them from Resurrection General. Their security is a little lax, but they'll spot that activity in routine audits of external traffic. Luka's security people will check out your email."

"Boy, will they be surprised." Stein chuckles. "Nah, I think Luka has a rough idea of who he's dealing with. He's getting worried."

"He's playing for high stakes. I want to give you some color on what you're looking at."

"Shoot."

"Luka is trafficking organs. I think they plan to cut up Rowan tonight. Her heart is going to fetch one hundred million dollars."

Stein gasps. "That much?"

"I heard Nurse Shelly and Dr. Durand conducting an

auction right in the basement of Resurrection General. The heart was a special order. A four-point match, whatever that is. Ask your pathologists—that must be what all the tests are for. They accept runaways and do complete work-ups on them. They take orders, and match bidders with donors."

"I'll speak with the best at Walter Reed."

"Please. They're making a hundred on her heart, but they're not letting her kidneys or liver go to waste. There are two kidneys to sell. Apparently, the liver has three lobes, and each lobe is viable for a transplant. Right now, they're having fun getting the best price for either a package deal or the pieces."

"My God, they're a cold-blooded bunch."

"It's not an urban legend anymore, Stein. Mark Luka has created a brilliant, if warped business model. Now, let's talk about Carmen Esposito. She's a special case."

"The girl who got run over."

"No question it was murder. Your pathologists should look at her autopsy report. She has ligature marks on her wrists and ankles. That means she was kept tied up for a while, probably with a thin leather cord or twine. I think it was restraint, not torture. Somehow, she got away and started running north. For some reason, they killed her rather than take her back. Whoever did it had a real mean streak. He hit her at sixty miles an hour and just broke her up."

"If she escaped and was killed on Old US 51, the odds are that she was held at Mark Luka's house."

"Exactly. We're seeing a triangulation of activity around that house. Esposito was killed northwest on 51. Bailey Mitchell and Taylor Purdy were found in the swamp at Resurrection Bayou. That's south by east."

"Rowan must be on Luka's Island."

"We can't afford to guess wrong. Find out what's required to execute this kind of operation. I'm not sure they're equipped to harvest organs at Luka's house. We all know the urban legend of the guy who gets fed the date-rape drug and wakes up in his hotel room—minus a kidney. I *hope* it's just a legend. Everything Luka and Durand need is at the hospital. If they have to do the work tonight, they might be holding Rowan there."

"You're sure they said tonight?"

"Absolutely. No *earlier* than nine o'clock, no *later* than ten. Apparently the heart is only viable for six hours, and they have a strict schedule."

"There's a very real problem here, Breed."

"Tell me."

"We don't have any *evidence* to arrest Luka. That video Ellie stole from Miriam Winslet is evidence against Des and Victoria Calthorpe, and not very strong evidence, at that. We have *no* evidence against Luka, and no time to organize a police raid at either location."

I'm not about to tell Stein that Luka is an *obayifo*, a human instrument of malevolent gods, sacrificing innocent children to advance his own greed.

"We don't need evidence, Stein."

"What do you mean, we don't need evidence?"

"Figure it out."

14

DAY THREE - LAKE PONTCHARTRAIN, 1400 HRS

Inside the general store, I take in the camping and hunting equipment. The racks of rifles on the wall, the boxes of ammunition on the shelves, the pistols in the glass cases. My attention switches to the hunting clothing and shelves of accessories.

I belly up to the counter and ask the shopkeeper for help. He's an elderly man with thinning white hair and glasses perched on a sharp nose.

"What can I help you with, sir?"

"I've got a list and not much time," I say. "Help me go through it?"

"I'll do what I can."

In half an hour, my items are piled on the counter next to his till. A gray Patagonia Gore-Tex windbreaker with fleece lining, Canon 15x50 weatherproof binoculars, a Surefire Tactician flashlight, a Cold Steel OSS double-edged knife, a Benchmade Claymore spring-loaded knife, a pistol belt, a holster for the SIG, and a canvas pouch for spare SIG magazines.

The shopkeeper bags the items, and I pay the bill. Carry the gear out to the Taurus and unlock the trunk. The Ingram I took from the gunman sits in its sack with half a dozen thirty-round magazines. A second sack with another half dozen magazines sits next to it. Those are heavy sacks. If you've handled a loaded 1911, you know how heavy eight rounds of .45-caliber ACP are. Imagine six thirty-round magazines for a total of one hundred and eighty rounds, plus the thirty in the weapon.

I snap open the Benchmade and cut the tags off the windbreaker. Shrug it on. Then I take the binoculars from their box and set them on the passenger seat. The Cold Steel goes into its scabbard, which I fit onto the pistol belt.

The Surefire, I unbox and slip into my left-hand jacket pocket. I close the Benchmade and slip it into my right. I walk the packaging over to a trash can at the end of the parking lot and dump it. Leave the Ingram, the pistol belt, and the Cold Steel in the trunk. The SIG remains in my waistband. Slam the trunk shut and get into the car.

FROM THE I-10 WESTBOUND, I take the Leblanc exit. I've left it a bit late, and I have to double back. The problem is the elevated highway. Much of it rolls over marsh and swamp. In some places, the highway is a bit below treetop height. One can look out to the right and see vast expanses of salt marsh and flat land that are easily flooded. Imagine floodwaters closing over the few roads that disappear forever when the waters recede. Katrina devastated this place. The waters crushed everything. The off-ramps are built close to roads and buildings that have survived over time.

Look to the left from I-10, and one can see patches of these surviving structures and new ones built close to them. It's as though the survivors have staked out safer ground. As buildings spring up, the clumps of civilization spread out and acquire a veneer of permanence. Yet deep down, one knows the impression of safety is deceptive.

I make my way to a road with a view of the lake and Luka's Island. There, I pull off the track where it runs closer to the tree line. Stop the car and get out, taking the binoculars with me.

A quarter of a mile away, Luka's Island appears to float on Lake Pontchartrain. Anyone on the island looking toward the shore will see the flat expanse of marsh and earth. Behind that, a line of trees and the I-10. My gray Taurus sits low to the ground against that backdrop. Hopefully, it will not draw attention from a casual observer.

I stand behind the car and glass the island.

There it is. The plantation-style house with two wings. I estimate the scale of the house. Height and width. I can't judge depth from this location, but that's okay. I'll change position later, and I've already flown around the house with Magellan Navigator. It's a powerful app that allows a user to explore any location on the planet in either two or three dimensions. It combines satellite photography, GPS, and meticulously constructed topographical maps.

I take a paper napkin and pen from my pocket. Lay the paper on the hood of the car and sketch the house. Use the pen as a paperweight and glass the house some more. I note key features, look for the house's inhabitants.

Four wide French doors on the ground floor, each flanked by windows. They open out onto a wide porch. There's a single window on the ground floor of each of the two wings. May well be more along the sides or the back, but these are what I can see. Of course, the plantation houses were designed to be airy and cool in hot summers.

New Orleans is built on a swamp. July and August are hot, humid, and insect-infested. Thank God this is late autumn.

The windows are shuttered.

Shuttered windows are unusual. The shutters are meant to protect the windows from storms and high winds. At this time of year, blinds are enough to ensure privacy, especially when you're sitting on an island.

A man walks back and forth on the front porch, smoking a cigarette.

Five windows form a row on the second floor. A single window in each of the wings. The roof slopes upward to two attic windows. The windows on the upper floors are also shuttered. I see seven chimneys. Three down the middle of the main house and two more in each wing.

The shuttered windows are definitely unusual. Especially because Mark Luka is in town. Does he want to live in a shuttered house? Maybe the lakefront windows are open. I don't have time to rent a boat.

It's palatial. I estimate the depth of the structure from the images on Magellan Navigator. I reckon the ground floor has ten rooms. Six in the main house and two in each wing. A similar number on the second floor, and four in the attic. There is certainly a basement.

Sweep the glasses over the bridge. It's wide enough for a car. The app showed me details of a carriage house. I saw it, partly obscured, when Kennedy drove me over I-10 to visit Carmen Esposito's murder site. The carriage house is obviously used as a garage and houses staff—Luka's private army of hitters. Behind the carriage house is a boathouse and a small wharf.

At the end of the bridge is a road leading away from the main house. There, on the shore, are another boathouse and wharf.

Lake Pontchartrain is no place for a super-yacht even though Mark Luka can afford it. He probably keeps one on the Gulf Coast. Here, he's got a thirty-six-foot, twin-screw pleasure boat with a shallow draft. Sleek and beautiful, with a molded composite hull. That baby probably does thirty knots.

Two men are standing in the well deck with their hands on their hips. They're looking down at something in the engine space.

That means there is at least one more man working on the diesels.

Four men, so far.

Turning my attention to the west, I see more marsh and swamp, another elevated highway. The elevated highway is the new I-55. Between I-55 and Luka's Island lies Old US 51, where Carmen Esposito was killed. It's not visible from my vantage point because it is at water level. It is literally obscured by marsh reeds and cypress forest.

I enhance my drawing to include the bridge and boathouse. Then I get back in the Taurus and use my phone to consult Magellan Navigator. I want to study Luka's Island firsthand. Magellan Navigator is updated on an irregular frequency. It is normal to find significant discrepancies between Magellan and the current lay of the land.

There are several roads that lead from Old US 51 to the

western edge of Lake Pontchartrain. Another road, like the one I'm on, parallels the waterline. I zip the phone into the Patagonia's vest pocket and start the engine. Pull a quick U-turn and head back the way I came.

I won't have to pass the spot where Carmen Esposito was killed. Half a mile north on Old US 51, I turn east on Frenier Road. It's paved, but not much more than a single lane. If I meet a car going the other way, we'll have to slow right down and edge past each other. There's a long string of old telephone poles along the left side. Landlines and power lines, a silent promise of rudimentary civilization at the other end.

Three-quarters of a mile farther, I find myself at a junction. It's the lake road that runs parallel to the lakeshore. I ignore it, drive a little bit farther on Frenier and find that the paved road disappears. I'm at the waterline, surrounded by marsh and swamp. There, ahead and to my right, is Luka's Island.

I get out of the car, take out my field glasses, and inspect the gangster's estate. It's as I thought. The arrangement of windows around the house is symmetrical. The windows on the ground floor are shuttered. Those on the east side of the second floor are open. Those must be Mark Luka's living quarters.

Carriage house, boathouse, wharf and bridge. Poles on the bridge carry the house's landline and power line.

I can see Carmen Esposito's escape in my mind's eye. How she slipped her bonds isn't clear. Those ligatures were tight enough that she couldn't get out of them without help. I think she was untied. To go to the bathroom, for exercise, or to be raped. Probably the last. Her guard or guards would have been alert otherwise. Only in the act of rutting would a guard be careless enough to allow the girl to get the better of him.

Esposito did exactly that. Somehow, she disabled him and ran out of the house. Crossed the bridge and lost herself in the swamp. I'll bet she more or less followed the lake road. It was faster than traveling through brush in the dark. She had to go down Frenier Road, guided by starlight or moonlight. There are no streetlights on Frenier Road. It is literally the sticks. But the trees are sparse. There is no canopy to speak of.

When she reached Old US 51, she turned north. She probably didn't know where she was. When her kidnappers brought her to Luka's Island, she was either unconscious or blindfolded. Had she known where she was, had she been properly oriented, she would have turned south. Had she turned south, help was only minutes away.

But she turned north and sealed her fate. It was twenty miles to Ponchatoula in that direction. Her kidnappers realized she was gone and split into two groups. One group headed south and the other north. The group that headed north caught up to her two miles up Old US 51.

I doubt they were instructed to kill her. She was worth money to them. But there is no shortage of psychopaths among men who do to children what these men did to Bailey Mitchell and Taylor Purdy. Whoever caught up to her on that dark road pinned the girl in his headlights. She saw him, knew she'd been caught, started running.

Wonder how far they followed her. A desperate figure, running on the dark road, chasing her own shadow. The one cast by the bright beams. Powerful LED lights that blinded her whenever she turned her head.

Until her lungs gave out, or her pursuer tired of the game. He stopped, let her get ahead, then floored the gas. Accelerated to sixty miles an hour and smashed into her. Ripped her open and broke her body with a two-thousand-pound automobile.

Who does that sound like?

I'M PARKED on the side of the road, phone in hand.

"What do you have for me, Stein?"

"All four children were tissue-typed," Stein says. "It's necessary to evaluate donors and recipients for organ transplants."

"Unusual?"

"Not necessarily. It has become common for people to donate their organs in the event of their death. The children probably signed something in their application when they checked into Miriam Winslet."

"Not all of them are of legal age to provide consent."

"That's true, but I'm unfamiliar with that area of the law. Miriam Winslet is a charity. By applying for shelter with Miriam Winslet, it's possible Miriam Winslet became their legal guardian. Don't quote me, Breed. We need expert legal advice on this issue."

"It's diabolical."

"They were only tissue-typed. The testing could have been legal. Remember, none of them were actually used as donors. They disappeared, and the bodies of Taylor Purdy and Bailey Mitchell were mutilated in a manner suggestive of ritual murder."

"Alright. Can Luka and Durand do the harvesting in Luka's home?"

"Yes, if they outfit an operating theater to do the job. I consulted a couple of surgeons at Walter Reed. They said it would not be hard to set up such a theater if one had the money. Especially since the donors are not expected to live. They have to be kept alive until the harvest is complete. Ideally, the heart is taken immediately following death. No later than thirty minutes."

I shudder at Stein's words. The cold-bloodedness of the criminals is beyond belief.

"The important thing," Stein says, "is to preserve the viability of the organs. There are considerable logistics to be dealt with. The organs have to be harvested and transported to the facility where the transplant is to take place. Depending on policies, procedures and legalities, certain documents have to be prepared. I've diverted my team to look at it. We think there is considerable forgery going on."

"Your team? But you're not officially involved."

"No," Stein says, "I'm not. And the CIA is not supposed to get involved in domestic operations. So far, it's a small resource ask, so I'm happy to do it. I can pull the FBI into the case at the appropriate time. Kidnapping and interstate transport of trafficked organs is their jurisdiction, no question."

"Alright. I'm convinced Rowan is being held on Luka's Island. I always thought the hospital was unlikely. It's too small, and it's crawling with people."

"Yes. One needs privacy for this sort of thing." Stein hesitates. "What now, Breed?"

"We rescue Rowan. But that island is a fortress. I need a plan."

ALBERTINE OPENS her door to me and smiles. "Breed, we have to stop meeting like this."

I take Albertine in my arms and kiss her. Enjoy the feeling of her supple body, the firm-soft sensation of her flesh under my hands. The sweet, humid space of her mouth, the taste of her tongue. She begins to move her hips against me, and I feel myself responding.

Gently, I separate from her.

"I need your help," I say.

Albertine's hazel eyes are all pupil. "What can I do?"

"I need Bastien and Rémy to help me get my friend's sister back. It's dangerous. We could be killed."

"The girl who was taken by the *obayifo*?"

I nod. "He's going to kill her. Like the other girl and boy."

Albertine looks down for a long moment, then back at me. "I will ask them. They will do it for me."

The girl goes into her living room and picks up her phone. Punches in a number. A gruff male voice answers. They speak together in Cajun French for several minutes. I hear the word *obayifo*. Finally, Albertine disconnects the call and looks back at me. "They are coming."

"Thank you."

"You can explain what you need when they arrive," Albertine says. "Now, I have something to show you."

The girl steps to a set of shelves against one wall of the living room. Takes an apple off the shelf and carries it to me in both hands. "Look at this."

"What is it?"

Albertine says nothing. She's sliced the apple in two with a razor. A circular cut about two-thirds of the way from the base. The cut runs completely around the fruit. Gently, she lifts the top off. The inside of the bottom has been scooped out, leaving a space. She's poured dark rum into it. For a second, I wonder if I'm supposed to drink it.

"Look closely," she says.

There—a piece of blue paper rolled into a tiny tube. It's set in the rum. Carefully, with two slender fingers, she plucks it from its receptacle. Hands it to me. "Read it."

Slowly, I unroll the paper and read the five letters printed on it in block capitals. It says *BREED*.

I tilt my head and lift an eyebrow. "What's this?"

"It's an offering to *Oshun*, the goddess of love and gold. I asked her to intercede on your behalf with *Legba*. To grant you peace."

Albertine takes the paper from me, rolls it up, and replaces it in the apple. Sets the apple back on the shelf.

I don't know whether to be flattered or amused. "You... cast a spell on me?"

"Not exactly. It doesn't work on *you*. Understand, *Legba* will do to you what he wants. I appealed to *Oshun* to ask him to stop."

"And he'll do it for her?"

"In exchange for something he wants from *her*. Yes."

"And she'll give it to him?"

"Yes. Because I am giving something of value to *her*."

This sounds simple. Why am I confused?

"What's that?" I ask.

Albertine looks sad. "That isn't important, Breed. At the

next ceremony, I will ask *Oshun* to enter me and complete the transaction. Do not worry about this anymore."

The certainty in Albertine's tone is disconcerting. The gods of *Obeah* give their flock what they desire... in a manner so transactional it smacks of deals with the devil. No cop-outs like "God helps those who help themselves" here. Pay what you owe and the gods of *Obeah* make good.

There's a knock on the door.

Albertine lets Bastien and Rémy into the room.

15

DAY THREE - LAKE PONTCHARTRAIN, 1600 HRS

Bastien's Ford pickup bounces down a rutted road west of Resurrection Bayou. It's not paved, and the other night's rains have gouged deep channels in the red clay. I worry the Taurus will bottom out, but heck, it isn't my car.

We find ourselves in a clearing. At one end is a house built of wood planks, crudely nailed together and balanced precariously on stilts. It was built on stilts to protect it from storm surge. Crates covered with rotting tarp have been stacked underneath. Chickens run free in the yard, clucking and beating their wings, dancing around white plastic lawn furniture.

Beyond the house, the bayou glistens in the late afternoon sun.

The pickup lurches to a stop, and the Cajuns dismount. "Come with me," Bastien says.

I climb out of the Taurus and push the door shut. The air is laced with dust and what can only be powdered chicken shit. In front of the house is a circle of rocks that surrounds a cold cooking fire. A rack has been constructed with a pair of cypress branches hacked down and cut to form Y-shaped posts. The posts have been buried five feet apart in the clay, and a crosspiece has been laid across them. Three great speckled trout have been hung from the crosspiece.

"Good fish," I say. They're fine fish. I'd be proud to have landed any one of them.

Bastien turns. For the first time, I see his eyes light up. "Good time of year," he says. "In the summer, too much fresh water. No salt in lake, no fish. When salt come back, they spawn."

I pass the fish and their dead eyes. There's the annoying buzz of flies. Not more than a handful, thank goodness.

We walk across the clay surface of the clearing. There's a stream behind the house that directs rainwater to the bayou. Tannin from the trees has stained the runoff the color of strong tea.

There's a table outside, behind the house. A small deer has been shot and laid on it. There's a wound the size of a golf ball over the animal's heart. No exit wound I can see. If that's the entry wound, it must have been some heavy-caliber rifle. The hunter hasn't begun the job of gutting and skinning his kill.

Another rack has been constructed and planted in the clay. Animal skins and pelts have been draped over the crossbeam.

The Cajuns lead me to the water's edge. There, dragged up onto the shore, are three flat-bottomed canoes of smooth black wood. Pirogues. They're each about fifteen feet long, with two sets of oars laid in the bottom.

"This only way to get on that island," Bastien says.

"They'll see us."

"We go at night. Lie down, flat to the water. They won't see anything."

These men are poachers. They make their money hunting and fishing in the bayou, and they're not shy about straying onto government preserves. That cannon Bastien carries can take down an alligator with one shot. A big python might take two.

Bastien turns around without another word and walks to the house. Rémy and I follow him. Clearly, the red-bearded man is the leader of the pair. We climb the rickety steps, and I cringe as the staircase sways under our weight.

Inside, the house is modest but comfortable. There's a kitchen with a white enamel fridge and stove that look like they were built in the 1940s. I didn't see power poles on the way in; Bastien must be stealing electricity from the main line that supplies Resurrection Bayou.

The fridge door has a rusty chrome-plated handle that works like a latch. Bastien grabs the handle and pulls it down like a lever. The latch unlocks, and the door springs open. The Cajun takes out three cans of beer and tosses two to us. Closes the fridge door and pushes the lever to make sure it's properly shut.

A pair of black mink pelts lies on a table. I'm not familiar with Louisiana fish and game law, but I'm willing to bet trapping season for mink is a couple months away. There are wooden shelves fixed to the walls. Stacks of canned goods. Alcohol burner, Coleman lamp in case the lights go out.

We drink cold beer together. Bastien goes to a workbench next to a grimy window. The workbench is stacked with ammunition-loading equipment. The most striking feature is a large turret-style reloading press. Other equipment is laid out in an organized fashion. Priming dies, case tumblers, a manual powder scale, buckets of spent shell casings... every tool has its purpose.

Bastien makes his own bullets. There's a supply of lead and tin and a single-bullet mold for the .43 Spanish—smaller caliber bullets can be cast in multiple-bullet molds. He has a melting pot and all the other materials and tools used to make ammunition.

We used to load our own in Montana. Once I joined the Army, there was no need. We relied on OPA—other people's ammo. Uncle Sam gave us all the thousand-round cases of ammunition we wanted. We'd go out and shoot three thousand rounds each on a Saturday. I'd shoot until my shoulder was bruised and my hands were quivering.

It's muscle memory. You learn the math and technical skills, but like any skill, practice makes perfect.

A mat of swamp moss has been spread on the floor next to the workbench. Piled on it is a stack of thin wooden boards, eight inches wide and a foot long. Four slits have been cut into each of the boards, positioned so they divide the wood into thirds, lengthwise. Thick rubber bands an inch wide have been run through the slits. The bands have been cut from the inner tubes of discarded tires.

Bastien hands me a pair of boards.

"What are these for?" I ask.

"You paddle with these," he says. "Lie in pirogue, you can't use oars. Use these and go slow so you don't stir a wake."

I get the idea. You stick your hands through the rubber bands. Lie face-down in the pirogue, paddle with the boards.

"Alright," I say. "We need to talk about what we're going to do when we get on the island."

"We kill the *obayifo*," Bastien says.
"Yes, but it is more important to rescue the girl."

THE SUN IS AN ORANGE PLATE, fractured by daggers of cloud drifting from the east. It's descending behind the line of cypress trees in the direction of the elevated I-55. I'm huddled against a trunk at the tree line southeast of Luka's Island.

Bastien and Rémy left me here an hour ago, with one of the pirogues. The canoe is hidden in a copse of trees thirty feet away, covered in brush. I scratched and clawed brush into a low barrier to conceal myself from Luka's men.

We drove down the lake road in Bastien's pickup, hauling two pirogues on a rattling old trailer. Drove right into the trees and unlimbered one of the canoes. Carried it down to the water. The two Cajuns helped me conceal the boat where it would be easy to launch after dark.

Our plan is simple. Well after dark, at eight o'clock, we'll make our way to the island. We'll lie flat in the pirogues and paddle quietly so as not to be detected. I'll land on the southeast side. Bastien and Rémy will land on the north.

I'll enter the house and rescue Rowan. Bastien and Rémy will cover me. They'll prevent Luka's men in the carriage house from interfering.

Everybody's got a plan until they get punched in the face.

A flock of geese soar across the sky, silhouetted against the setting sun.

The men working on the speedboat climb out and stand on the wharf. Light up smokes and crack open beers.

At my feet lies the canvas sack with the Ingram and ammunition. I've put all the spare Ingram magazines, twelve in all, in the bag. It's heavy, but the Ingram's rate of ammunition expenditure is prodigious. I've got the pistol belt buckled over my shirt and I've got the SIG and Cold Steel blade in a holster and scabbard. The spare pistol mags lie in a pouch on the pistol belt, and the Benchmade dagger sits in my jacket pocket.

I reach into the sack and take out a can of beer. Crack it open, lean back and wait.

ONE OF THE men on the wharf slaps another on the shoulder. Raises his hand and points at me. I almost choke on the beer sliding down my throat. Freeze, squint at the scene on the wharf.

He's not pointing at me. He's pointing at something to my left, about a hundred yards west along the tree line. There are shouts. A man in the well deck throws a rifle to the men on the wharf. It's an AR platform. One of the men puts his arm through the rifle's sling, takes aim, and fires.

Another rifle is thrown to the men on the wharf. One of them takes off running down the drive toward the lake road. The other two jump down from the wharf to the shore and run along the tree line and into the woods. The man in the boat climbs onto the wharf to guard the bridge.

Damn, what were they shooting at?

It's hard for me to make anything out. It's getting darker, and the shadows are long. Whatever's going on could ruin everything. They're running right toward me.

No reason to panic. The pirogue's well hidden. I sit quietly, searching the tree line.

There.

I catch a glimpse of white. A slender figure in a light-colored jacket running along the tree line, then ducking into the woods. There's more light on the shore, but there, the girl is an easy target. She has to get behind cover and concealment.

She's running toward me, and two of the men are chasing her. One of them runs into the woods and the other runs along the tree line. He's not worried about being shot by his friend on the wharf, and he can run faster on the shore.

I watch his progress carefully. He'll be making up ground on the girl. She had a head start, but she's running more slowly in the woods. His friend, running closer to the lake road, is also going to be hampered by the darkness and difficult terrain.

I remain still, breathing slowly. In and out, in and out. Only my eyes move.

Figures crash through the brush toward me. The girl runs past. She misses me by all of three feet without seeing me sitting there. Then the man with his rifle. He's running with the rifle at high port, gasping for breath. Charges right by. Where's the other guy?

The second man is well back, maybe a hundred yards. He hasn't made up any of the girl's head start.

I rise to my feet and follow the girl and the first man. Leave the haversack and Ingram behind.

There's a thump, and I hear a grunt. One of them has fallen.

It's the girl. She's sprawled on her belly. Turns to look up. The guy is right in front of me, sucking wind from the effort of running. He stops, raises his rifle, and takes aim. The girl raises one hand like her palm can stop a bullet.

I clap my left hand over the guy's nose and mouth at the same time I draw the Cold Steel from its scabbard. Pull his head back so his eyes are staring at the cypress canopy and the night sky.

With one motion, I plunge the point of the Cold Steel dagger into the side of the man's neck. The point and four inches of double-edged steel emerge from the other side. I punch the blade forward and sever all the man's plumbing with one stroke. He drops the rifle, and I hold my hand over his mouth while he gurgles his life away.

I drag the dead man into the trees and hide him under some brush. Retrieve his rifle and help the girl to her feet.

It's Ellie.

The damn kid is going to ruin everything.

I silence her with a gesture, guide her another fifty yards. Maneuver close to the shore, pull her down next to a clump of trees.

She starts to say something, but I hush her a second time. Make her lie on her side. I drag some brush toward us, then lie down next to her. Pull the brush over us like a blanket. "Stay quiet," I tell her in a low voice. "Don't move."

I hear the second man advancing through the forest. Crushing vegetation under his feet. The man swears under his breath because it's getting too dark to see. I'm counting on that to buy us time. The sounds he's making recede in the direction of the road.

He's gone. Decided not to make his way back through the forest. It's creepy walking around in the dark if the dark isn't your friend. He doesn't know where his buddy is, and he isn't happy tramping around the woods alone. He's going to return to the bridge by way of the road.

Ellie's breathing has normalized. I draw the SIG, put my arm around her to hold her still.

Minutes pass. Ellie stirs and shifts her position. Her arm must be going numb. She folds her arms and lies on her shoulder. I turn a bit to allow her room to move.

A low thrumming issues from the lake and grows in volume. A brilliant white light stabs the night. I squint through the brush that conceals us. The speedboat is crawling slowly past our position. It's a long shadow lying low to the water, bearing a high-power searchlight.

I tighten my grip on Ellie's shoulder. She freezes, lies perfectly still.

The searchlight is mounted on top of the cockpit, just ahead of the boat's antennas. It's controlled remotely from inside, and it's systematically sweeping the shore. It swept the waterline for fifteen yards, then swept the tree line in the opposite direction for fifteen yards. Back and forth, back and forth. The boat is cruising thirty yards out. It's got a shallow draft, and this part of the lake is not too marshy, but the men are taking no chances.

Two shadowy figures sit in the well deck. They're scanning the shore, their gaze tracking the searchlight. Both carry rifles. They've given up chasing her through the trees. One of their men went missing. They have no idea what happened to him, but they have to assume he's come to no good end.

They were chasing a slip of a girl. They didn't hear more than the single shot they fired. That meant the girl might have company. Mark Luka's organization has already lost twelve men. They have to bet I'm out here.

Another engine sounds from our right. This is louder, noisier, a high-pitched whine. Another boat is making its way slowly toward the bridge, playing a searchlight around the tree line. This is an airboat, with an extremely shallow draft. With its engine and fan raised above the waterline on its stern, there's no danger of getting fouled in the marsh. A man sits in a high open cockpit, piloting the boat. Two men sit on the passenger couch at the bow, manipulating the searchlight. They are armed with rifles.

The airboat is new. My earlier reconnaissance didn't pick it up. They must keep it in the boathouse, for use in areas of the lake that are particularly marshy. This boat is cruising fifteen yards out. Much closer to shore than the speedboat.

The speedboat makes its way to the bridge, then turns and makes another pass, crawling four hundred yards up the shore. The searchlight sweeps over our position again, but we're low to the ground, under concealment, and well inside the tree line. When the boat passes, I relax my grip on Ellie.

When the speedboat draws even with the airboat, the two boats stop, and the crews speak. Then the boats continue their search.

At the end of its traverse, the speedboat gears up and speeds away. Its twin screws kick up a shining wake as it races around the island. We wait for it to return to the shore. Instead, as soon as the boat's frothy wake is out of sight, the crew cuts the engine. They're tying up at the island's wharf.

The airboat reaches the bridge, turns sharply and speeds away. It makes a turn around the island, then returns to the landward boathouse.

I sit up. Push the brush away, lean back against a tree trunk. I holster the pistol, remind myself to go back for the Ingram. I'll do that on the way to the pirogue.

Ellie sits up and brushes herself off. Our eyes have adjusted to the darkness, and we can make out each other's features. I check my watch. Forty-five minutes left to get the pirogue into the water. I by God want to spank the brat.

"We've got time," I tell her. "How did you get here?"

Ellie takes a deep breath and tells me what happened after I put her on the bus.

16

DAY THREE - LAKE PONTCHARTRAIN, 1900 HRS

Ellie is uncomfortable talking about how she defied me by returning to New Orleans. Too bad. I need to get caught up on what's happened. She might have information useful in the coming hours. I listen as she recounts her story.

ELLIE WAS HEADING BACK into the belly of the beast. Breed had put her on the bus to Pensacola. Like a bad penny, she'd gotten off at Mobile and immediately bought a ticket back to New Orleans. It was no good arguing with Breed. She knew he was right, but it was not in her nature to sit on her hands. When she got off the Greyhound, she immediately set off for the Garden District.

Ellie stepped off the St. Charles Avenue streetcar at Jackson Avenue. It was a bright morning in the Garden District, but already she could see hints of cloud and an overcast that would creep in by late afternoon.

She walked west on St. Charles, past the Indigo Hotel. Turned left, crossed the wide, tree-shaded avenue, and passed the half-dozen buildings of the Louise S. McGehee School that bordered the avenue. Warren had gone several blocks farther when he drove her to Miriam Winslet. When she made her escape from Des, she had cut through the school, emerged between these buildings, and jumped the fence.

The streetcar ran twenty-four seven, but she'd chosen an ungodly hour to make her escape. The service ran so infrequently at four o'clock in the morning that she'd done better to walk out of the neighborhood.

In the darkness, she wasn't able to fully appreciate the beauty of the school buildings. In broad daylight, she was impressed by their varied architecture. Here, a beautiful Greek Revival, there, a row of centuries-old houses. Once owned by wealthy families in the Garden District, now converted to administrative offices and classrooms.

On the other side of the fence, Ellie saw girls her age walking to class. They were cheerful and clean, dressed in gray-and-white plaid skirts and blazers. The sight brought a wistful ache to Ellie's heart. If only she and Rowan could find such a place where they could belong. She knew it wasn't going to happen. Already, her path had diverged from that of those happy girls.

Ellie pushed the dream from her mind and walked past the school. Forced herself to concentrate on the task at hand. When she came to the traffic light where Warren had turned off St. Charles, she clenched her fist and walked toward Miriam Winslet.

She knew the layout of the Miriam Winslet property. Des occupied the carriage house, and she needed to know where he was. She walked past the front of the property. The minivan was in the drive. The Jeep Cherokee might be in the shop, or it might be concealed in the garage.

No sign of Des.

She walked around the block. Both the big house and the carriage house were set back from the front fence by about thirty feet. The carriage house was two stories and a third of the length of the big house. The backyard was huge, with magnolias and a well-kept lawn shaded by spreading oak trees. The wrought-iron fence circled the property.

Ellie didn't linger. She walked back to St. Charles and Jackson Avenue. Continued east past a number of nice hotels and events venues, found a comfortable patisserie. Sat down for breakfast. After an hour, she bought a pair of ham and cheese croissants, packed them into her haversack, and walked back to Miriam Winslet.

The minivan was gone.

Ellie did a turn around the block. A full three-sixty. There was no activity visible in the big house. Without hesitation, she jumped for the fence. Grabbed the top rail between the ornamental spiked posts and threw her right leg over. Found purchase and pulled herself up. Balanced herself on the rail for a second, then lowered herself on the inside.

She hung for a moment, then dropped to the ground and jogged to the carriage house. The lock on the back door yielded to a five-dollar plastic gift card. She swung it open and let herself in.

There was a long corridor with the front door at the far end. A stairway on the left led from the front door to the second floor. Under the staircase immediately to her left was a storage closet and an interior door that opened to the garage.

Ellie opened the garage door. The Jeep Cherokee sat in the dim light. Its front bumper had been crushed by its impact with the sacks of cement. The windshield was a spiderweb of cracks.

Back into the hall. Another interior door to her right. She opened it carefully, found herself in a workshop. The place smelled of wood and varnish. A large pegboard covered one wall. Hanging from the pegs were two dozen hammers of different sizes, a dozen saws of different types and sizes, electric drills and looped power cords. Beneath the pegboard were shelves and drawers that contained more tools.

There were two worktables. One was fixed to the wall, next to the shelves. Another table was wheeled and could be repositioned at will. There was a heavy-duty band saw in one corner, and wood sawhorses.

Ellie went to the front end of the workshop. Stepped through another interior door and found herself at the foot of the stairway. She steeled herself against a surprise. Perhaps Richard had taken the minivan, and Des was upstairs. Told herself that was unlikely and climbed to the second floor.

As she approached the landing, Ellie hesitated. There were walls on both sides of the stairs that restricted her field of view to left and right. Straight ahead, she could see an open dining space, kitchen, and bedroom doors to the right.

Ellie took a breath and peeped around the corner to the left.

The second floor was spacious. There was a living room with a sofa, wing chairs, coffee table, and TV set. From the stairs, she had seen the dining space, kitchen, and two bedrooms. Windows looked out on the driveway and backyard.

One bedroom wasn't in use. The bedroom windows looked out toward the big house. Ellie scanned the house for activity, saw nothing.

Between the two bedrooms was a shared bathroom and shower. Empty.

Ellie went to the other bedroom. Swung the door open and found it belonged to Des. There was no mistaking the distinctive male smell in the air. He didn't have many belongings. A queen-sized bed, with a nightstand and chest of drawers. There was a table pushed against one wall for use as a desk. A straight-backed chair. A closet with a collection of work and casual clothes.

Ellie went to the nightstand and opened the drawers in succession. Folded T-shirts, rolled socks, folded underwear. Underneath the underwear were a passport, cash, a pistol, and a box of ammunition.

The pistol was a snub-nosed revolver. The titanium-gray barrel wasn't more than two inches long. Black frame, titanium-colored cylinder, polished wooden grip. The weapon was compact. Squinting at it, Ellie counted eight shots. She could see the round noses of seven bullets from the front. Another was lying under the hammer.

Ellie held the gun in her right hand. Placed her thumb on the hammer spur. She wasn't familiar with guns, but how difficult could it be? She pulled back slightly on the trigger, tested it against its spring. The cylinder started to move. Okay, if you pulled the hammer back all the way, you advanced the cylinder and cocked it.

She eased the hammer down and tested the trigger with her finger. Found that pulling the trigger caused the hammer to draw back and the cylinder to advance. Okay, if you pulled the trigger, it advanced the cylinder, automatically drew back the hammer and fired.

So there were two ways to fire this pistol. One way was to pull the hammer back and then pull the trigger. Another was to pull the trigger. Simple. Both looked pretty safe. Ellie didn't think the gun could go off so long as the hammer was down and you didn't pull the trigger.

There was a small lever on the left-hand side of the frame. It was easy to reach with her thumb. Ellie didn't know what it was for, but she decided to test it. She kept her finger away from the trigger and thumbed the switch. The cylinder came loose and swung open. It spun on a spindle, and she saw the backs of eight bullets nestled snugly in their chambers.

Ellie swung the cylinder back into place, felt the switch click under her thumb.

All good. She placed the revolver in her jacket's right-hand pocket.

The box of ammunition slid open. It was labeled *50 Cartridges .357 Magnum 158 Grain JHP*. She put the box back in the drawer and slid it shut.

No idea when Des would get back. She went into the living room.

Ellie knew what she wanted to do. She'd thought about it on the bus and in the patisserie. At the time, she didn't know what the inside of the carriage house looked like, so the details needed to wait until she got inside.

As it turned out, the arrangement wasn't so different from what she had in mind. There was the living room area and the dining area. The dining area had a table for four and four straight-backed chairs. All would suit.

The stairs came up from the first floor. Their view of the living room was restricted by one living room wall and the side of the hall closet.

Ellie checked her watch. She didn't know how much longer Des was going to be. She hurried down to the workshop. Took two long coils of extension cord off the pegboard. From the tools, she selected a suitably heavy C-wrench. Hefted it in her hand.

She didn't want to kill him.

Ellie carried the extension cords and wrench back up the stairs. Set the cords on the sofa, then went into Des's bedroom and took a T-shirt from his drawer. Tied it around the head of the wrench until it formed a pad to cushion the force of a blow.

If she didn't knock him out, she might well have to kill him.

The revolver was heavy in her pocket. Could she do it? Des had tried to kill her. Rowan might be lying murdered in a swamp. Ellie would do what she had to do.

An engine rumbled in the driveway. Ellie stepped to the living room window, peeled the curtain aside an inch. She had a clear view of the minivan pulling into the driveway. Des parked the vehicle, got out and closed the gate.

The handyman stepped to the front door and unlocked it. Ellie lost sight of him when he entered the carriage house. She picked up the wrench from the sofa. Stood next to the landing, at the edge of the living room wall. Should she hit him in the face first? She'd actually prefer to hit him in the back of the head. She listened for the sound of Des climbing the stairs.

Nothing. She heard the sound of the door to the workshop opening. Des went inside and puttered around. Ellie's heart beat like a trip hammer. Her palm was sweaty on the wrench.

There was a creak as Des mounted the stairs. Ellie shut her eyes as his footsteps approached. He was bigger than she was, stronger than she was. She remembered hitting her father with a baseball bat all those years ago. She hadn't planned that—it just happened. Somehow, attacking Des was different. More cold-blooded. She wasn't sure she could do it.

Des was close. He was on the other side of the wall. He stepped onto the landing and into the living room. Caught sight of her in the corner of his eye, whipped around to face her.

Ellie hit him as he turned. His height made a difference—a full head taller. Ellie had to reach up to hit him. She swung the wrench with all her strength. There was a thud as it made contact with his left temple. The impact almost knocked the wrench from her hand, never mind she was gripping it like the tool owed her money. His head snapped to one side, and he seemed to stumble. He went down on his right shoulder like a falling tree. Rolled onto his back, stared at her with glassy eyes.

She didn't know what he was seeing through those eyes. Threw herself on him, swung and hit him again in the same place. Her whole body was on fire. She raised the club again, ready to swing, but his eyes had closed.

Ellie stood up, sucking air through parted lips.

Des was unconscious or dead. She had little idea how to

tell which. Not for sure. She knew how to take her own pulse. Reached down and put her hand to the side of his neck. Nothing.

Damn! She didn't *mean* to kill him.

She felt the other side of his neck. Nothing.

Got on one knee and felt his wrist. Nothing. Squeezed harder, closer to his thumb.

There! Something moved under her fingers. One of his veins, twitching like a worm. Relieved, Ellie struggled to her feet.

Alright, she had no idea how long he'd remain unconscious.

It was time to go to work.

ELLIE SAT on one of the straight-backed dining chairs, waiting for Des to wake up. He was sitting opposite her in another chair. His ankles and knees were tied together with an extension cord. His wrists were tied behind his back, around the back of the chair. For good measure, she'd bound his elbows together. Stuck a pair of socks in his mouth.

She held the wrench in both hands. It dangled between her legs.

Des groaned.

Ellie leaned forward. "Hey."

Des groaned again. Shook his head as though to clear it and stopped. He must have been feeling a terrible headache. His eyes opened. When he saw her, they widened.

"I'm glad you're awake," Ellie said. "I'm going to ask you some questions. If you don't answer, I'm going to hurt you until you do, okay?"

Des roared from behind the gag, threw himself against his bonds. Ellie gritted her teeth and swung the wrench against his left kneecap. He roared louder and fell back in the chair. Twisted left and right. Tears came to his eyes.

"Don't make me do this," Ellie said. "I'm not very good at it, and I don't want to kill you by accident, okay?"

Des slumped in his chair.

"I'm going to ask you questions. If you want to answer, nod your head. I'll take the gag out. If you try to scream for help, I'll knock your brains out. Got that?"

Des nodded.

"Okay. Where's Rowan Miller?"

The man sat still, stared at the wrench in Ellie's hand.

"Where's Rowan Miller?"

No response. Ellie got up, wielded the wrench with both hands. Brought it down on his other kneecap. She was surprised by the crack—the wrench was still covered by the T-shirt. The impact must have shattered his patella.

Des howled from behind the gag. Or at least, Ellie imagined the sound would have been a howl if the socks hadn't muffled it. He jerked and twisted like an insane puppet. Ellie was so unnerved by what she had done that she took a step back.

"See what you made me do? Now tell me where Rowan Miller is."

Des sobbed and shook his head violently.

Ellie gritted her teeth and swung one-handed at the left side of his face. The force of the blow almost clubbed him from the chair. He would have fallen over had his arms not been bound behind the chair back.

"Tell me. I'm starting to enjoy this."

Des nodded drunkenly.

"Okay," Ellie said. "I'm going to take the gag out. If you try to call for help, I'll have to knock you out again. Don't try anything."

The gag was harder to remove than she'd expected. Two socks, one crammed well behind his front teeth and the other kind of curled up, sticking out and hanging from his mouth like a black tongue. She pulled on it until the one sock came out, then stuck her fingers in to pull out the other.

Des hollered at the top of his lungs. "Help!"

Ellie swung again, one-handed, and hit him on the side of his jaw. His body rocked sideways and the chair almost tipped over. A pair of red-and-white dice rattled on the floor. Ellie was shocked to realize she'd knocked out a pair of his teeth. Bloody spit drooled from his mouth and onto the front of his shirt.

"Tell me. If you live, I swear you'll never be the same."

Damn. If she broke his jaw or shattered his skull, he wouldn't be able to tell her anything. Ellie looked around. Of course she couldn't see through walls, but she hoped no one had heard him shout.

"That's enough," Des gasped. "She's in Mark Luka's house."

"Why? What do they want with her?"

"I don't know."

"You know they killed Taylor and Bailey."

"I don't know anything about that, I swear. My job, *our* job—me, Richard and Jasmine—is to keep an eye on the kids for Victoria. When the time comes, we turn them over to Luka's guys. That's all I know."

"How much longer has Rowan got?"

"I don't know."

"Where's Mark Luka's house?"

"It's that big house on Lake Pontchartrain, out toward Lake Maurepas."

"Open your mouth."

Des opened his mouth. Ellie set the wrench down on her chair and stuffed one of the socks back behind his front teeth. Reached for the other sock to finish the job.

The blow surprised her. Somehow, while she was knocking him around, Des had managed to work his right arm free. He punched her in the side of the face, and she lost her balance. She was too close for him to throw much momentum into the blow, but it stunned her. He grabbed her with the free hand and pulled her close.

He stared at her with mad eyes. Yelled from behind the gag. Tried to push the sock out with his tongue. Ellie tried to reach the wrench, but he was holding her too close. He was jerking like a maniac, trying to pull his other arm free. His right hand clutched at the back of her jacket, then her left arm. His fingers dug deep into the flesh over her bicep.

Des's left arm came free, and he held her in a bear hug. His legs were still bound, but he had both arms around her, pinning her arms to her sides. He was crushing her to him. If he let her go, she'd grab the wrench and hit him again before he could free himself. Their embrace was almost comical, but Ellie was terrified.

The terrible stalemate lasted barely thirty seconds. Upper arms pinned to her sides, Ellie was nose to nose with Des. She stared into his mad eyes while bloody spit drooled from around the gag. She reached into her pocket, found the pistol, and tried to draw it.

Des was crushing her—holding her so tightly that she couldn't get the revolver free of her pocket. She shoved it against his left rib cage and pulled the trigger. Double-action, it was a long, six-pound pull. Smooth. She was surprised when the gun went off. She shot him through her jacket pocket.

Des's body muffled the gunshot like a silencer. The shot wouldn't have been audible outside the carriage house. Des's eyes widened with shock and pain. Ellie pulled the trigger a second time. Both rounds went into the man's chest cavity. His grip tightened on her, then relaxed, and his head slumped over her left shoulder.

Ellie fired a third time. Des's arms fell to his sides. She pushed him back in the chair and his chin slumped onto his chest. Ellie stumbled backward, drew the pistol and extended the weapon. She wondered if she should shoot him again in the head. Breed always did that. "Anyone worth shooting once is worth shooting twice," he'd told her. Well, she'd already shot Des three times. She sat in her chair and stared at the dead man.

She didn't know it at the time, but she was lucky she had shot Des with a revolver. Had the pistol been an autoloader, pushing it against Des's body might have thrown it out of battery. It wouldn't have fired. Had it fired, an autoloader might have fouled inside her pocket.

Ellie forced herself to get to her feet. Ran to Des's bedroom and looked out the window. The big house was quiet. She ran to the living room's front window and looked out over the drive. There was no one there. A white SUV cruised down the street and disappeared from view. The oak leaves rustled in a gentle breeze.

Slowly, Ellie turned to survey the dining room.

Des was slumped in his chair.

The juice in her blood was gone. The adrenaline that had perfused her muscles was wearing off, diluted by fresh blood pumped by her racing heart. Ellie was left shaking. Not just her hands—her whole body trembled like she was possessed. She grimaced, fought down the bile that rose in her throat. Squeezed her eyes shut.

That wasn't supposed to happen.

Ellie straightened, picked up her haversack from the sofa, and slung it over her shoulder. She went to the bathroom, checked herself for blood, and examined herself in the mirror. Her jacket was spotless, but there were three clean bullet holes in her right pocket. Too small for anyone to notice. The same couldn't be said for Des. The bullets had punched holes in his shirt. The powder flare that had scorched the *inside* of her pocket left burns around the holes in his shirt.

The house was full of her fingerprints, but she wasn't about to worry. Stein had cleansed all national databases of Ellie's biometric data under every one of her identities. Ellie took the box of bullets from Des's drawer and tossed it into her haversack. Did another turn around the second floor to make sure she didn't leave personal items behind. Then she hurried down the stairs, opened the back door, and climbed over the back fence.

Fifteen minutes later, she walked down St. Charles to Jackson Avenue. There was the rumble of the streetcar's wheels, the click of the car's catenary. She liked the picturesque green carriages, their brown doors and brown trim around the windows. They were all vintage originals, over a hundred years old. The streetcar stopped, and she hauled herself aboard and bought a ticket.

The interiors were well-maintained, the paneling polished woodwork. The slatted wooden seats were shiny with varnish. The seat backs could be flipped with brass handles so passenger groups of four could face each other. Seats could be reversed for the return trip. The huge windows allowed a panoramic view of the avenue, and a number had been opened wide to let in a gentle breeze.

Ellie found herself a window seat halfway down the streetcar on the right-hand side, facing the direction of travel. Made herself comfortable. Jammed her haversack on her right between her body and the elegant wood paneling. The revolver was snug in her pocket. She stared out the window and watched the Garden District roll by.

She had to find Mark Luka's house and plan her next move.

Ellie rented a car with her gold-plated Stein-provided ID. Got into the red Honda Civic and set her haversack on the passenger seat. She'd never driven a car, but she'd watched people drive all the time. It wasn't hard to figure out the rules.

She started the car, shifted into reverse, and pulled out of the parking space.

The attendant yelled, "Whoa!"

Ellie hit the brakes, and the car lurched to a stop. She'd turned too soon and nearly scraped the next car in the lot.

"Watch it," the young man said. "Straighten your wheels, back straight out. I'll tell you when you can turn."

The attendant was a helpful kid. Ellie wasn't a sweet girl by nature, but she tried her best to smile as the gallant knight guided her out of the space. "I think I've got it now," she said.

Ellie shifted into drive and made her way off the lot. In

the rearview mirror, she saw the young man staring after her, shaking his head.

It was midafternoon, and clouds were intruding on the blue sky. Ellie wanted to find a coffee shop where she could study a map and find Mark Luka's house.

She thought of calling Breed, but dreaded his anger. She didn't know where he was, or what he was up to.

Ellie was going to find her sister first. Only when she was absolutely sure she had found Rowan would she call Breed.

I stare at Ellie. Her eyes are shiny in the dark. I would have done the same in her place. There wasn't any point coming to me with half a story. "Alright," I say, "tell me how you got here. Exactly."

17

DAY THREE - LAKE PONTCHARTRAIN, 1930 HRS

I'm proud of how Ellie handled herself. I didn't want her in town for the rough stuff, but she's done what I would have done in her position. The question is, how did she get here? I don't want to miss a detail that might prove important later. I listen for land mines as she continues her story.

MAGELLAN NAVIGATOR IS one of Ellie's favorite apps. She located Mark Luka's house and used the software to fly around the island. She looked straight down and examined it in two-dimensional view. Did a full three-sixty in three-dimensional view. She dropped down to water level and studied the island from every direction. Took tens of screenshots to study.

Ellie was well aware that Magellan Navigator was good, but was not necessarily up to date. She knew she had to reconnoiter the island. Struggled to program the address into the Honda's GPS system. Then, for good measure, she took a piece of paper from inside the glove compartment and drew herself a map leading from I-10 to where she figured she could get a good view of the island.

Driving onto the freeway was one of the most horrifying experiences of her life. She coaxed the Honda Civic onto the on-ramp, hesitated, drew a blast from the car horn of the driver behind her.

Ellie gripped the wheel so tightly her knuckles showed bone-white. Stamped on the accelerator and rocketed forward. Looked over her left shoulder and saw cars coming at her like stampeding bulls. She floored the gas and raced into the traffic.

She glued herself to the rightmost lane all the way to the turn-off. Made her way to Old US 51 and Frenier Road. Like Breed, she drove straight past the lake road to the water's edge. Got out and stepped into his tire tracks without realizing it. She studied Luka's Island.

It was impossible to get the kind of detail Ellie wanted without binoculars. All she knew was that getting onto the island wouldn't be easy.

What would Breed do? Parachute in. Swim underwater with a hit squad. Find some crazy kid to show him an underground tunnel.

Sorry, Ellie had none of that. Unless she was willing to swim for it, she had to get across the bridge. It was the only way. She got back in the car, turned around, and drove back to the lake road.

There were a lot of trees around Frenier Road and the lake road. She found a large copse set thirty yards back from the junction and drove the Civic straight into it. When she could see neither the trail nor the road, she turned the engine off. Flipped open the cylinder of her revolver, made certain she'd replaced the three rounds she'd fired into Des. Then she got out of the car, shrugged on her haversack, and locked the vehicle.

Ellie was operating on the principle that if you couldn't see *them*, they couldn't see *you*. She walked to the lake road, turned south, and followed the tree line to Luka's Island. She walked slowly, stayed close to the trees. Should a vehicle come upon her on the road, she would hear it coming. She'd have time to take cover.

The sun was going down. Ellie worried that she was running out of time.

Half a mile farther, she came to a paved turnoff that led to the lake. The pavement was concrete as opposed to the cracked asphalt. It was new and well-constructed. There were no signs, but it had to be the turnoff to Luka's Island.

She couldn't stroll down that road. That led to the landward boathouse, the bridge, and lakeshore parking for the estate. Ellie kept going another two hundred yards down the lake road before ducking into the trees and making for the waterline.

The view from the waterline was excellent. She was close enough to see the island, the bridge, and the boathouse. She crouched at the water's edge, studying the construction of the bridge and the wharf. The wooden pilings.

Nice boat. Must have cost a pretty penny. But it was too big for the boathouse, used to stash smaller boats. In front of the boathouse, at the foot of the bridge, was a broad concrete parking space. There were three vehicles in view. A blue Taurus sedan, a gray Jeep Cherokee, and a white Toyota Land Cruiser.

Three men climbed from the speedboat and onto the

wharf. They stood there and lit up cigarettes. A fourth man standing in the back of the boat tossed them cans of beer. They stood talking casually, watching the sun go down over the swamp.

Ellie worried about getting to the island. She doubted the men slept on the boat, and the boathouse didn't look accommodating. They probably lived in the carriage house. But where would they post guards, if at all? Would they guard the shore or the island side of the bridge? Either would make it impossible for her to cross.

She might have to swim for it. If she had to, she would.

One of the men threw his head back to drain his beer, crushed the can, and tossed it into the swamp. When he looked up, he was staring at her.

Ellie froze. Eyes are drawn to motion. Maybe he hadn't seen her and his gaze would sweep on.

No such luck.

He slapped the shoulder of the man next to him and pointed at her.

Ellie faded back against the tree line.

Shit. What to do?

If she ran back to the car, she'd pass the concrete drive. They might have someone waiting for her. She decided to run in the other direction and put some distance between them. She could find a place to hide.

THE MAN in the boat threw a rifle up to the men on the wharf. One man caught it, put his arm through the sling to use as a brace, and took aim. *Crack.* A bullet whacked into a tree trunk behind her.

Two more men with rifles jumped from the wharf onto the shoreline and started running toward her. The fourth man ran up the drive. Sure enough, they were going to block her retreat to Frenier Road.

Ellie ducked inside the tree line and started to run. She crashed through the foliage, pushing aside branches that grasped at her like claws. Twilight was upon the bayou, and the forest was darkening.

Sweating, breathing hard. She couldn't tell how far back the men were. The shadows were so deep it was becoming impossible to see where she was going. She fought the temptation to make her way to the shore, where it might be easier to run. It was only a few feet away, but on the shore she would be visible from the bridge and the island.

Cypress roots snaked everywhere. The forest seemed to be alive, clutching at her with twisted claws. It was impossible to run and think at the same time.

Ellie tripped on a root and sprawled on the forest floor. Heard movement behind her, rolled over. Found herself staring up at one of the men from the wharf. It was dark and he was a shadowy figure staring down at her. His rifle was raised, ready to fire.

A second shadow detached itself from a nearby tree. Stepped behind the man with the rifle. Clamped a hand over his nose and mouth, pulled his head back. A long, eight-inch blade flashed in the dim light. It plunged straight into the side of the man's neck and emerged from the other side. A swift movement, and a black spray burst from the front of the man's throat.

The man with the knife dragged his victim away. When he returned, he'd replaced the knife in its scabbard.

Breed.

"Is that everything?" I ask.

"You know the rest," Ellie says.

I check my watch. Fair is fair, and I tell Ellie what I've learned, spare her nothing. Tell her about Shelly and Durand auctioning Rowan's heart. Ellie listens, fist clenched.

18

DAY THREE - LAKE PONTCHARTRAIN, 2000 HRS

Ellie's eyes glitter in the dark. "I'm coming, Breed. Don't try to talk me out of it."

What am I supposed to do, tie her up? Every time I tell her to stay away or go home, she comes back like a dog that won't leave her master. This time, she nearly ruined the mission. Luka's hitters will be on high alert.

"You can come. But you do exactly what I say. Exactly."

I hand Ellie two boards with inner-tube straps. "Paddle in time with me. No splashing."

We slide the pirogue into the water and wade in after it. I set the sack and the Ingram in the middle and hold it steady while she gets in. I climb in after her and lie down. There's just enough room for us to lie end-to-end.

It's a dark night. The clouds that were creeping in during the late afternoon have blocked out the stars. I look across the swamp at the plantation house. I'm looking for signs that Luka has posted sentries on overwatch in the attic, but all the windows on the landward side are shuttered. I see the faint glow of lights coming from behind shutters on the first floor.

There's no movement at either end of the bridge, but that doesn't mean no one's there. We saw six men in the boats. It makes sense that Luka would pull them in to the island rather than leave some hanging on the landward side. That's why they moored the speedboat at the island wharf.

The bridge is lit by lamps mounted on the phone and power poles that run the length of the structure. The lights are reflected in the obsidian glass of the swamp. On the island side of the bridge, there's a driveway next to the west wing. Two sedans are parked in the drive. Behind them lie the wharf and the speedboat. Partially obscured by the west wing is the carriage house.

The windows of the carriage house are lit. Luka's servants and hitters certainly live there. How many? Six men on the boats, less one. At least five. There's light coming from the west wing. Not necessarily from windows. I remember from my afternoon reconnaissance that those were shuttered. There's probably a nightlight mounted on the outer wall.

I push off gently and start paddling.

The paddle-boards allow us to generate a lot of force. I'm careful to slide the boards into the water slowly at the start of each stroke, pull hard, then lift them from the water cleanly. I set a slow, steady pace. A fast pace would splash and generate a frothy wake. Ellie pulls with me.

A man steps out from behind the east corner of the house and walks slowly along the front. He's carrying a rifle, looking out over the water, right at us. His gaze sweeps past, travels to the boathouse at the end of the bridge.

I keep paddling, look to my left and right. I notice what

look like logs lying in the water, just off the shore. Alligators, for God's sake. If the men have done this kind of sentry duty before, they could mistake us for an alligator.

Another man steps from the right corner, and the two meet in the middle, just off the porch. They stop to exchange words, light up cigarettes. Then they continue on their way, walking in opposite directions. One circles the house clockwise, the other counterclockwise.

The island and the house tower over us as we approach. The place was built to survive storm surge and heavy flooding. That's why the bridge and house are built fifteen feet above sea level. At the waterline, the island is concrete and rock, covered by earth as one approaches the house.

"It's got to be haunted," Ellie whispers.

I say nothing, but I know exactly what she means. The plantation house looks like the kind of place an *obayifo* would use to conceal the ultimate in depravity. It's not hard to imagine those walls echoing with the screams of murdered children.

The pirogue makes landfall with a soft bump. I roll out of the boat, grab the sack, and sling it over my shoulder. I beckon Ellie forward. When she's joined me on the island, I push the pirogue off into the swamp. If the sentries notice it pulled up onto the island, the game will be up. They may think nothing of another log floating in the swamp.

We pick our way up the slope. The footing is treacherous until we encounter earth. Even then, I feel no confidence. When we reach the plateau where the house is built, I lie flat, and Ellie lies next to me.

None of this is ideal. I want to dispose of the sentries separately. The worst time is when their paths cross. I have to wait until they've separated, and one of them is out of sight on the other side of the house. Then, ideally, I want to take one down from behind.

One of the men approaches from the side of the house closest to the bridge.

I push Ellie down. The man walks past, and I draw the Cold Steel from its scabbard. I get to my feet and approach him from behind as he walks past the front porch.

Hurry past the shuttered windows. Up close, I clearly see the glow of electrical light bleeding from around the protective wooden panels. Pass the porch and the thick wooden pillars supporting the second-floor balcony.

I'm almost on top of the sentry when he turns. His mouth opens to shout, and I chop the edge of my left hand across his throat. Smash his voice box. Slam him hard against the nearest pillar, clamp my hand over his nose and mouth, pin his occiput against the wood.

Thrust the Cold Steel into the bottom of his jaw. The blade passes through the soft tissue inside the horseshoe of the lower mandible, then punches through the soft palate. I follow through and crunch the thin bones at the base of his skull. The point sinks into his frontal cortex and I twist the blade as I lift him off his feet. Impaled, he convulses. His limbic brain shoots electric impulses down the long nerves to his extremities. His bladder empties, and his heels drum against the pillar before he goes still.

I jerk the knife from the man's head. As he crumples, I take his rifle and set it down.

No easy way to do this. I push the body to the edge and roll him down the incline. Damn! He rolls halfway down and gets hung up against a rock.

Ellie creeps forward. Reaches for the man's shirt, drags

him over the rock, and sends him on his way. He slides into the water with a soft splash.

I melt back into the shadows at the side of the house.

The second sentry steps into view and looks around. His friend is nowhere in sight. The man goes to the edge and stares down at the water. It's dark, and he's trying to discern shapes that conform to the irregular outline of the rocks on the slope. The only thing down there that has straight lines that look man-made is the pirogue.

I'm not about to wait for him to figure things out. Step forward, catch him from behind. Clap my left hand over his nose and mouth, draw him close. My knife goes up under his breastbone, slices through his diaphragm, and pierces his right ventricle. The razor-sharp blade impales his heart, and the point exits through the left atrium. I twist the blade around to destroy as much of the muscle as possible. Slice up the aorta.

The man goes limp. I draw the knife from his body, relieve him of his rifle, and kick him over the side.

I wave to Ellie to join me. She scampers up the incline, and I pull her to the side of the house.

Check my watch. It's eight forty. We're cutting it fine, but we can save Rowan.

We have to find the house's electric meter. Power comes in from the mainland, over those poles rising from the bridge. The bridge is on the west side of the house. The power will come through the meter and down to the switchbox inside the west wing.

I listen for sound coming from the north side of the house. Nothing. If everything has gone to plan, Bastien and Rémy have made it onto the island. They'll be in position to interdict rescuers coming from the carriage house. That's important because the boathouse, the wharf, and the parking lot are on the west side where the bridge is.

If I have to work on the west side of the plantation house, we'll be easy to spot from the drive. There's also more light coming from the lamps on the bridge, the windows of the carriage house, and the night-light on the wall of the west wing.

There. From the corner of the west wing, I can see where the phone and power cables come in. They're stretched high over the drive, fastened to the side of the house. From there, they will run down to ground level.

I motion Ellie to hang back. "Keep that pistol in your pocket," I tell her. "I don't want you shooting me by accident."

Peer around the corner. All the utilities enter the house from this spot. I can see a pair of meters against the wall. The larger one looks like a round clock face. The other is smaller, connected to steel pipes. That will be the water meter.

"Stay here," I tell Ellie. "Don't move."

Pressed against the wall of the west wing, I make my way to the meters.

Hate this. I'm bare-ass naked out here. I'm barely thirty feet from the carriage house. Facing the meters, I'm standing next to shiny Mercedes and Taurus sedans. But the cars are parked in line. They're not screening me from the carriage house. I can see shadowy figures moving behind the windows.

Parked behind the plantation house, hidden from the landward side, is Sheriff Kennedy's police cruiser. I should have guessed. There's nothing like having a cop along when you've got depravity afoot. Is she in the carriage house or the plantation house? I reckon we'll find out.

Get on with it.

I squat and examine the meter. It's a hard plastic dome about ten inches in diameter that covers the instrumentation. There are barcodes on its face. The dome is held in place by a thin metal ring with a slot and wire tab. The ring has a shoulder along its circumference that engages a lip on the edge of the meter and the rim of the meter socket. It holds the meter in the socket. The ring's tab has been passed through the slot and sealed to indicate tampering.

I reach into my haversack and take out a rolled-up rubber mat. Spread it on the ground below the meter and step on it. This should be a straightforward job, but I don't want to fry myself by accident. The meter is advancing, which is exactly what I expected. There are hot loads in both the plantation house and carriage house.

Kids, don't try this at home.

There's a pair of wire cutters in my haversack for exactly this purpose. I take the wire cutters and snip the tab. Spread the ring and remove it. I have to push it up so the cover can clear the meter. This is the scary part. Metal components under the cover have current flowing through them.

The minute I kill the power, all hell will break loose.

I don't know where in the house Durand is performing surgery on Rowan, but he's going to have a hard time doing it in the dark. Equally important, all the medical equipment he's using will die without power.

What kind of team will he have with him? An anesthesiologist, certainly. But if Rowan's survival is not required, Durand can operate with a minimalist setup. He may even administer the anesthesia himself. All he needs to do is ensure that Rowan is alive until the harvest. Ideally, the heart must be harvested no more than thirty minutes after death.

Once the harvest is done, we've seen what the sick Dr. Durand likes to do with his donors.

Behind the meter, the power transmission cable and the house cable are each attached to a pair of contact blades. They're designed to snap into a pair of metal jaws in the back of the meter. The jaws are stiffly sprung. Not a good idea to have those contacts come loose. When the blades are firmly seated in the jaws, a circuit is completed, and power flows from the city transmission line, through the meter, to the circuit box inside the house. When I pull the meter free, that circuit will be broken.

One of the little things they teach special operators. How to kill power to a house from the *outside*.

Check my watch. It's eight fifty.

Hang on, Rowan. Cavalry's on the way.

If you're careful to *not* damage the meter, you rock the device back and forth until the jaws are pulled off the blades. After all, the meter belongs to the power company. They get upset if you break it. They ask you for money.

I, on the other hand, don't give a shit. Count to three, rip the meter off the wall with one heave. All the lights on the island go out and I fling the meter into the swamp. It doesn't quite have the distance. Lands on the rocks near the waterline and shatters. No one's plugging it back in tonight.

The carriage house door swings open, and two men come out, looking around themselves. Both are carrying rifles.

A gunshot splits the night air like the blast from a cannon. Bastien's Remington rolling block. The first man's chest explodes like a grenade went off inside it. Those home-made lead bullets don't overpenetrate. They squash flat, punch a lot of pressure into that half-inch space, and create a massive wound cavity. The overpressure in that cavity is so great, a lot of its contents explode backward through the entry wound.

The second man tries to duck into the carriage house. There's a flat crack—a .30-30 slug from Rémy's rifle hits him in the back.

Six men in the two boats. I've killed two, and the Cajuns have killed two. That means Luka has two hitters and Sheriff Kennedy somewhere on the island.

Time to go to work.

19

DAY THREE - LUKA'S ISLAND, 2100 HRS

I draw the SIG from its holster and the Surefire from my left jacket pocket. Slip my wrist into the lanyard of the Surefire. Dodge around the corner of the house and bound up the stairs to the thirty-foot-wide front porch. Advance on the front door. It's sturdy oak, opens inward. I rattle the doorknob, find it locked.

Ellie crouches behind me, left hand against the wall for balance. I motion her to stay where she is.

I turn, bend over, and mule-kick the door. Once, twice. It bursts open, and I step to the right. Hold the pistol in my right hand, rest my right wrist on top of my left. My left hand holds the Surefire. I thumb the flashlight's plunger switch, and its beam stabs the darkness.

Left corner is clear. I shift left and check the right corner. Clear.

Push into the center hall. There's a cavernous living room to the left, an equally vast sitting room on the right. Two different decors. There are similarly large rooms on either side to the back of the house. Libraries.

There's a footstep behind me. Ellie, Smith revolver in hand. The girl's instincts are good. She follows close behind, looking left when I look right.

Mahogany furniture hundreds of years old squats on the sitting room floors. I swing the Surefire's beam from one side to the other. Realize the two sitting rooms are furnished with pieces from different centuries. Mark Luka, the nouveau riche gangster, has acquired impeccable taste. The room on the left is furnished in eighteenth-century New Orleans, the room on the right is furnished in nineteenth-century Plantation.

There's an original Louis XV writing desk. In some ways, the items don't appear to be integrated with Luka's personality. It's like he acquired them to impress people. Had an interior decorator go to town. The place looks like a movie set for *Interview with the Vampire*.

There's no time to clear the whole house. When you're in a hostage-rescue situation, your first job is to find the captive you're there to rescue. If you fiddle and fuss doing everything by the rules, people end up dead.

If Luka has built an operating theater for Durand in this house, it'll be in the basement. I need to find the stairs. I try to remember the makeshift floor plan I sketched of the plantation house.

I cross the living room on the left. There are two smaller rooms next to the living room before you reach the hallways that lead to the west wing. I see a passage that leads into one of those rooms. SIG raised, I enter.

There, to my left, is a staircase that plunges into stygian gloom. Another staircase rises to the second floor.

Like corridors, staircases are fatal funnels. If you get trapped in the middle, you have nowhere to run. You clear them as quickly as possible and get off the X. I move to the right corner of the wall that leads into the stairwell, flash the Surefire down the stairs.

My beam pins a hitter standing at the bottom. It's like shining deer or gators. I squeeze off a double tap that hits him in the face. He drops like he's been clubbed to death.

That leaves one hitter and Kennedy. Where are they?

I run down the stairs, pistol and Surefire raised. Light spills from around the edge of the door. I release the thumb switch on the Surefire, and the flashlight goes dark. I push into the room, and I'm greeted by a scene from a horror movie.

The basement is huge. It's got the same surface area as the living rooms and libraries above. The load-bearing walls run along the sides. The lack of a center wall creates a vast open space. The basement has been sunken deep into the concrete cap of the artificial island.

Luka built this house from scratch. He didn't renovate an existing building. He had plans drawn up and built everything brand new.

The ceiling, walls and floor are tiled. In the middle of the open space is an operating table. Sturdy steel, with other tables on trolleys arranged around it. There are metal tables pushed against the walls of the room. The lights mounted on stands that point down on the operating table are dark. The light in the room comes from four Coleman lanterns. Two have been set on trolleys next to the operating table. Another two have been set on wooden tables next to the walls. The light from the Coleman lanterns reflects from the shiny tile walls. It is like Luka to be prepared. In the event of a hurricane that kills power to the house, he wants a backup source of light.

The trolleys are set with trays covered with glittering steel instruments sharpened to perfection. Scalpels and surgical knives. Retractors, rib spreaders, and medical chisels. Tools of depravity.

There are five figures in the room.

A thin teenage girl is lying face-up on the operating table. It's Rowan. Her pale body is covered with rough green sheets. Bare feet, bare arms. Purple ligature marks circle her wrists and ankles. Just like Carmen Esposito. The cloth is arranged to leave the white flesh of her chest and belly exposed.

Rowan's mouth is open. An endotracheal tube inserted into her throat leads to a rubber breathing bag and ventilating machine. Nurse Shelly sits at the head of the table. The nurse is rhythmically compressing the bag. The ventilating machine died with the power, and Shelly has to manually breathe the girl to keep her alive.

The girl's eyes are open, and she's staring at Shelly. It's then that I realize she's paralyzed, but conscious. She can neither move nor speak nor scream. She cannot even breathe on her own. That's the horror the doctor has been inflicting on his victims. He dissects them while they are paralyzed but able to feel pain.

Rowan is aware of her surroundings. She feels everything that is being done to her. The cold air on her arms and feet, the rough sheets on her bare skin, the hard plastic tube crammed between her teeth and down her trachea. When the surgery begins, she'll feel the pain of every cut, every tug, as pieces are lifted out of her.

Standing over Rowan, gowned and scrubbed, is Dr. Emile Durand. He wears latex gloves and holds a scalpel raised in one hand—like a conductor's baton. Light from a

Coleman lantern gleams off the surgical steel. The instrument casts a towering black shadow against the wall.

Durand's attention is on Rowan's pale skin, where he is about to make an incision. While her heart is still circulating blood to keep them fresh, he'll take her liver and other organs. The doctor will save the heart for last. When that comes out, Rowan will be granted a merciful death.

Far to the left, in the shadows, is a uniformed figure. Sheriff Kennedy. That hard face has lost all attractiveness. It's as cold as a wall of granite.

Behind Durand is Mark Luka, dressed in casual clothes covered by operating room scrubs. On the floor next to him is a red-and-white ice chest with a biohazard symbol on it and big block letters that announce HUMAN ORGANS FOR TRANSPLANT.

That's all it takes. You do a bit of cutting, unplug the organ from the donor, and put it on ice. You can use a beer cooler. Six hours later, your one-hundred-million-dollar heart will be plugged into its new owner.

Durand looks up from Rowan's torso and meets my eyes. Stares at me through his round, wire-framed glasses. The light from the Coleman lantern throws his long, angular face into sharp relief. In the hospital, he looked clinical and dispassionate. Now, he confronts me with a demonic, malignant visage. The prospect of opening the helpless girl's body has stirred his passion and brought him to life.

The concentration of evil in this dungeon is suffocating.

For an instant, the demons stand like images seared into my retinas.

Luka bolts for another doorway to his left. The house is a wonderfully symmetrical design. Beyond that door lies another staircase that leads up to the east side of the plantation house.

Kennedy raises her pistol.

Durand's scalpel looms over Rowan. I fire three times. One of his circular lenses shatters as a bullet drills his eye. The second round hits him in the bridge of his nose, and a black halo erupts from the back of his head. The doctor crumples, and my third shot blows off a patch of scalp as he goes down. The blade tinkles on the floor.

There's the blast of a gunshot from behind me. Then another. To my left, Ellie is firing her revolver one-handed, arm extended. Natural point shooting at very close range. Her shots hit Kennedy in the shoulder and chest. The sheriff staggers.

I turn and put a bullet into the sheriff's forehead. Ellie shoots her twice more in the chest and throat as she collapses. The sheriff's pistol clatters to the floor. She's dead before she hits the ground. I point at Shelly and yell to Ellie, "Watch her! Make her work that bag!"

Run across the operating theater after Luka. I can hear the gangster's pounding footsteps as he climbs the stairs three at a time.

The stairwell's dark. I shine the illumination from the Surefire up the stairs. Luka, a ghostly figure in the flashlight beam, leans into the stairwell and points a weapon down the stairs. There's a crackle of gunfire. Pistol caliber, extremely high rate of fire. An Ingram.

I'm blinded by the muzzle flash, duck back into the operating theater. Bullets stitch the wooden paneling in the staircase.

Can't afford to wait. I hear the ring of metal on the floor as Luka dumps his mag. I charge up the stairs, rapid-firing the SIG. Keep him ducking. When I get to the landing, I sweep the Surefire over the sitting room.

He's gone. Left the front door swinging open.

I run to the front door and step onto the porch. Catch a glimpse of Luka running around the corner of the house.

Will Bastien and Rémy get him? I don't hear any shooting coming from the carriage house. The carriage house has only one entrance and one exit. The Cajuns have Luka's last man bottled up. They might already have killed him.

Luka's running to the wharf. I do a combat reload and go after him. There's a boom from Bastien's rolling block. A pair of cracks from Rémy's .30-30. The bullets smash holes in the side of the speedboat. Luka throws himself into the well deck, crawls forward to the cockpit.

I run for the speedboat, carrying my own Ingram and the sack of ammunition. The diesels start with a throaty roar, and fumes burst from the exhaust. Luka spins the wheel, gives the speedboat gas, pulls away from the wharf. In seconds, he's tearing across the lake.

If he runs straight west, he'll run into the shore that abuts the Old US 51. Where his men murdered Carmen Esposito. If he runs north, he'll head twenty miles across the lake to Ponchatoula. It's far more likely he'll head east toward New Orleans, where there are a million places to hide along the shore.

Sure enough, Luka turns the wheel and executes a sharp turn that puts the speedboat on its side. When he's got it pointed east, he opens up to full speed.

A man like Luka will have half a dozen different identities, a dozen homes, many places to hide. I have to get him now.

I turn around, wave to Bastien and Rémy. Point to the wharf across the bridge. They know what I want to do. Luka's hitters didn't store the airboat in the boathouse. They wanted it readily available to resume their search in the morning. The airboat is sitting tied up to the wharf.

Luka's speedboat goes thirty miles an hour. The airboat is really an airplane, flying along the surface of the water on an aluminum flat-bottom hull. That airboat can probably make a hundred miles an hour.

I clamber onto the airboat and climb onto the pilot's cockpit. There are two bucket seats. The pilot sits on the left with a steering stick at his left hand and the throttle and engine instrumentation on a podium on his right. There's a passenger couch on the lower deck.

The Ingram and ammo fit on the bucket seat to my right. From what I can tell, piloting an airboat is not much different from piloting a light plane. I turn my Surefire on the instrumentation, select the starter, and push it.

The engine roars to life, and I take out the Ingram so I can reach it. Then I go down to the lower deck and cast off. By the time I'm back in the pilot's seat, the engine has spun up to a high-pitched whine. There are ear-protection muffs behind the instrumentation panel. I pick up a pair and fix them over my ears.

The boat is a flat-bottom sled with a high-powered fan mounted aft. The fan is covered by an aluminum screen. The twin rudders aren't under water. They are right behind the fan.

I take the control stick in my left hand and test the controls. Look back. Sure enough, moving the stick left and right causes the rudders to move. My right hand falls comfortably on the throttle.

First time for everything, no time to waste. I push the throttle forward gently and maneuver the airboat away from the wharf. I do a sharp turn and accelerate toward the island. Pass the wharf, get out onto the lake, turn east.

My eyes scan the dark night. Luka's running two diesel screws that will throw up a heck of a wake.

There—I see him. Heading east, like I thought. Making for the shore in the direction of the Lake Pontchartrain Causeway. That's a long bridge. Must be twenty-five miles.

I can't see the causeway. The problem with Lake Pontchartrain is that it's plagued by fog. Fog moves. It creeps in at all hours, starts in one place and turns up somewhere else two hours later.

The Lake Pontchartrain Causeway should be visible, but it isn't. Instead, I see a wide, sweeping fog bank rolling toward us from the east. It's enveloping the shore, and Luka's heading right into it. The gangster slows down.

Dealing with the fog is risky, but it's my chance to catch up to Luka. I push the throttle and race faster. The whine of the fan, muffled by my earpro, reaches a crescendo. The airboat rips across the water of the lake at high speed. I'm going so fast, the flat bottom is barely touching the water. The pilot's cockpit is open, and I squint into the wind that lashes my face.

Luka's speedboat is swallowed by the fog bank. Before the fog rolled in, I saw a boat launch facility on the shore. It's possible Luka will make for it and continue his escape on dry land.

The fog engulfs me. It's cold, damp and smells of brine. The Gulf lies twenty miles away. Right time of year, right winds, they say you can smell the shrimp. I allow the airboat engine to idle, and the craft coasts, propelled by its forward momentum. Listen for the thrum of the speedboat engines.

Nothing. Luka might be playing the same game.

I reach for the Ingram and set it on my lap. Ahead, I see the hazy features of the boat-launch facility.

Drift past the wharf, look left and right. I strain to distinguish shapes obscured by curling white and gray tendrils. Colors are muted. Pilings, drums, ropes and life preservers on the wharf appear at various moments, then disappear. The curtain parts briefly, reveals a building set back from the lake. A second later, the curtain closes, and the wraith is gone.

From behind the cold, gray screen, the hull of the speedboat rears up in front of me. I'm going to glide right into it. I crank up the engine and throw the airboat to the left. Muzzle flashes twinkle like fireflies from the side window of the speedboat's cockpit. Luka's aimed low. Maybe all he can see is the flat deck of the airboat. Bullets stitch the passenger couch. I speed away and hide in the fog.

Luka revs his engines. They start to beat and rise to a steady thrum.

The fog smells like an open grave. One of us won't be going home tonight. I have never known evil like Mark Luka. *Obayifo*—he who steals the children.

The speedboat tears past me into the fog, heading east. He must be crazy, it's a chicken run. I lean on the throttle and accelerate after him. This is insane. In pea soup, I'm going faster than he is. We're both heading toward the Lake Pontchartrain Causeway. The bridge is probably closed because of the fog.

We're gambling we'll see the pilings in time to steer between them. I'm running even with the speedboat, Ingram in my right hand. I control speed by the friction of my fist against the throttle's Bakelite knob. Fog swirls and eddies around us as we charge forward at thirty miles an hour. I can barely make out Luka's well deck. I strain to see his cockpit. The plexiglass windows.

There. I aim low and hold down the trigger. Muzzle climb carries the stream of rounds into the cockpit's side windows. Two seconds, and thirty rounds shatter the plexiglass. I lean on the stick, back on the throttle. The airboat turns away in a tight arc.

Luka's speedboat keeps right on going. It's hard to say, but I don't think there is a living hand on the controls. The speedboat disappears into the fog, charges toward the causeway.

There's an earsplitting thunderclap that penetrates my earpro. A column of fire climbs one of the causeway's pilings and shoots into the sky. The fog swirls, smeared black, orange and crimson. The scene is a beautiful watercolor.

20

DAY THREE - LUKA'S ISLAND, 2200 HRS

I make my way back to Luka's Island in the airboat. Pull my phone from its pocket and dial Stein.
"We've got Rowan."
"Is she alright?"
"She's been drugged. We need paramedics at Luka's Island. We need an FBI team at the island, another at Miriam Winslet, and another to secure Resurrection General. They can arrest Victoria Calthorpe at Miriam Winslet and Karen Shelly on the island. Calthorpe is a glorified administrator. Des was one of Luka's hitters. I think *he* killed Carmen Esposito."
"What makes you think that?"
"He tried to run Ellie down with a Jeep. Carmen Esposito was killed in a hit-and-run."
"I'll have the special agent in charge meet you at the island and you can fill him in. I'll call you back."
That's Stein. Flawless at setting priorities, one hundred percent efficient.
My phone buzzes. "Hi."

"Hi." Stein's tone is crisp. "Special Agent Tom Morgan will be looking for you. He'll have a team of agents and paramedics."

"Thanks."

"What happened to Luka?"

"He was trying to get away in a speedboat and ran into the Lake Pontchartrain Causeway. I reckon he's been cremated and his remains are scattered all over the lake."

"You have anything to do with that?"

"Indirectly, yes."

I'm approaching Luka's Island. My eyes quarter the terrain, looking for signs of Bastien and Rémy. I'm starting to worry about Ellie and Rowan, even though I've only been away half an hour.

"I shot Dr. Durand before he could cut Rowan. Ellie shot Sheriff Kennedy before the sheriff could shoot *me*."

"Good lord. Where did she get a gun?"

"That's another thing. Ellie shot Des Krainer in the carriage house of Miriam Winslet. She made him tell her where Rowan was. He got loose and tried to kill her. She shot him with his own gun."

"Ellie's spending too much time around you."

"You think? Anyway, she took his gun. An eight-shot Smith & Wesson 327. I reckon she left fingerprints all over the place, so your people will have to sanitize it."

"That's not a problem."

I tie up the airboat on the island. The wharf is close to the carriage house, and one of Luka's hitters could still be alive. I don't hear any shooting.

Bastien and Rémy walk onto the wharf to meet me. I cruise up to the wharf and throw them the mooring rope.

"Are they all dead?" I ask.

"They not going to be around no more," Bastien says.

"That's good. Has the house been quiet?"

Rémy nods.

"Okay. You guys had better leave. The FBI is coming, and you don't want to have to answer a lot of questions. I'll take care of it."

The Cajuns walk to their pirogue, climb in, and paddle away.

Men of few words.

I go inside the plantation house and walk down the stairs to the operating theater.

"Ellie, it's Breed. Put that gun up."

"It's all good, Breed."

Ellie sounds tired.

I walk into the operating theater. Ellie is sitting on the tiled floor, cradling Rowan in her arms. The pistol is in her right hand. She's holding it on Shelly.

Rowan's awake, but looks terrible. She's as thin as her sister, but Ellie is rosy-cheeked with vitality. Rowan looks gray. Both girls are slim, but where Ellie is lissome, Rowan looks emaciated.

The paralytic has worn off. Rowan is breathing on her own, but she is lying like a rag doll in Ellie's arms.

"What did you give her?" I ask Shelly.

Shelly sits quietly, refuses to answer.

"The FBI will be here in half an hour. I reckon I can do anything I want to you in that time."

"You wouldn't dare."

I cock the hammer and point my SIG at Shelly's knee. "You're going to prison as an accessory to kidnapping and murder. Unfortunately, I don't think electrocution applies in your case. So I'm going to make sure you never walk again without a crutch."

Shelly looks away.

This 226 trigger has a three-pound single-action pull. A nice, clean break. There's a crack, very loud in the confined space of the operating theater. Shelly's knee explodes with a spray of blood and bone. The nurse screams and falls from her chair. She rolls around on the floor, clutching the shattered knee. Smears her dirty blood on the shiny tiles.

I adopt a teasing tone. "Tell me, tell me."

"A paralytic." Shelly writhes on the floor. "A curare derivative. He didn't tell me what it was."

"What kind of anesthesia?"

Tears flood Shelly's face. "He didn't give her any. He said the paralytic was all she needed."

"Do you believe her?" I ask Ellie.

Ellie shrugs.

"I don't think Ellie believes you," I tell Shelly. "I'll have to blow out your elbow."

"No. Please. I swear there was no anesthesia."

"Because you wanted her awake to experience everything. You were here when Durand gutted Taylor Purdy, weren't you? And Bailey Mitchell. You kept them awake and alive while he sliced them up. You and Durand are beyond evil."

"He wanted to make it look like Voodoo."

"*Obeah*. But Durand has a surgical fetish. Luka rapes them. Durand dissects them while they're alive. *You* like to watch. I'm going to kill you for that."

Shelly sobs.

I press the muzzle of the pistol to the side of her head. The metal is hard against her skull.

"Please! I don't want to die."

What a sick, miserable creature. I thumb the decock lever, drop the hammer with a click. Shelly jerks. Weeping, she presses her face against the floor.

"I shouldn't. But I think I'll let you live."

Ellie asks, "Will Rowan be okay?"

"She's breathing on her own," I say. "That's what's important. But we should get her to a hospital."

"*Not* Resurrection General," Ellie says.

21

DAY FOUR - TULANE MEDICAL CENTER, 1000 HRS

I ask for Rowan at reception. The well-groomed middle-aged woman at the desk lifts an eyebrow and makes a phone call. I was expecting something like that.

"Five north," the lady says.

The elevator isn't too much of a milk run. We let people off at two and three. I'm the only one who gets off at five. The elevator door sucks open, and I'm met by a dapper young man in a two-piece Brooks Brothers suit. The jacket's been cut to conceal a firearm. He looks too young to shave.

"Mr. Breed?"

The man checks my ID and returns it. Gestures toward a large pair of beige-colored butterfly doors marked 5N.

I step through the doors. There's a nursing station with a nurse and receptionist. There seem to be no patients on the ward. There are two men on the left wearing dark blue tactical gear. No police insignia, no FBI insignia. They are carrying H&K 416 carbines and SIGs in open holsters. These are Ground Branch. Stein's people.

One of the men holds up a hand, palm toward me. "Can I see some ID?"

Stein has this ward locked tight. I hand the operator my wallet and show him my armed forces card. The man nods, hands the ID back to me. "End of the hall on the left," he says. "You can't miss it."

I can't miss it because there are another two Ground Branch operators in front of Rowan's room. They repeat my ID check. One of them knocks on the door.

"Come," a woman's voice says.

The operator opens the door and shows me in.

It's a bright, airy room. The windows look out on a bright, sunny day in New Orleans. Stein is sitting at the foot of the bed. She's dressed in her signature black suit and flat black shoes. "You're looking well, Breed," she says. "No worse for wear."

"That's the wear you can see," I tell her.

Stein hesitates. She's not used to me being this real.

Ellie is curled up on a visitor's chair by the bed. She gets up and hugs me.

I disengage and gently guide Ellie back to her seat.

Rowan is sitting up in bed. The ghastly gray hue in her complexion is gone. She's not as rosy-cheeked as Ellie. Now she's only pale. The ligature marks on her wrists are an angry purple.

"Ro," Ellie says, "this is Breed. He and Stein are friends."

That's something. Ellie has a definite antisocial streak. For her to call someone "friend" is a big step.

Rowan shakes my hand. I'm surprised by her handshake. Not *strong*, but *firm*. There's a difference. There's a lot of Ellie in this girl.

"I don't remember very much," Rowan says.

"Did they give you drugs over the last few days?" I ask. "I mean *before* the operation."

"They made me take pills, but I don't know what they were."

Durand and Shelly probably had her on antipsychotics. A pharmacological restraint to make her docile prior to the main event.

"The paralytic has worn off," I tell her, "but that other junk can sit in your system for a couple of days. Don't beat yourself up. It'll come."

"Okay."

"Some of it," Ellie says, "you won't *want* to remember."

"The doctors are taking regular bloods," Stein says. "They'll monitor the levels of medication in your system. These things have half-lives. The amount of time it takes for half the original amount to clear. The point is, the doctors will give us chapter and verse on how you're doing. They're telling me you're in as good shape as can be expected."

Rowan doesn't look fazed by Stein's use of technical terminology. Instead, a sharp look of acuity comes to her eyes. Her intelligence is on par with Ellie's.

Ellie and Rowan. Intelligence and capability beyond their years. Emotionally, thirteen and sixteen years old. Blessed and cursed. I suppose time will catch them up. The important thing is to catch them up without breaking otherwise fragile spirits.

Stein nods to me. "Breed, can we speak?"

"Sure." I get up and say to Ellie, "We'll leave you girls for a bit."

I follow Stein into the ward. The Ground Branch operators stand aside and take flanking positions on either side of the door. Stein leads me down the corridor. I'm surprised the entire ward is deserted. She had it cleared for her special patient.

"Have you confirmed Mark Luka's death?" I ask.

"Yes. A body was fished out of Lake Pontchartrain. Burned beyond recognition. We got a match through dental records."

"Calthorpe and Shelly are little fish," I say. "We took out hitters, but not management. What's the story with the rest of Luka's organization?"

"The FBI is working on it. That's why the security. Rowan is still a witness to something. I doubt she knows anything that will impact Luka's organization. In fact, we'll probably get more out of the records at Resurrection General."

"That makes total sense. I reckon the FBI will be able to roll up the whole organ-traffic network."

Stein turns to me. "Breed, there's something else."

"Tell me."

"They did a full workup on Rowan when she was admitted. She was raped."

I was afraid of that. "Does she remember?"

"She hasn't brought it up. The paralytic has worn off, but the doctors found high levels of benzodiazepine in her blood. She was probably on it when she was raped. It will take time to clear her system."

"I bet that's how Carmen Esposito escaped. Luka untied her, but she wasn't on a pharmacological restraint. Managed to get away."

"They learned," Stein says. "They drugged Rowan so she wouldn't struggle while she was being raped."

"Will she remember?"

"We're moving ahead slowly. She'll get the best treatment we can provide. I'll have her meet an abuse psychologist.

What Ellie said is true. It might be better if she doesn't remember."

I wonder if *Legba* will torture Rowan in her sleep. If he does, maybe Albertine can help her.

"What about Ellie?"

"One step at a time. Ellie's identities need to be vetted and re-established. Rowan isn't going home, and I doubt she's going into the system. We need to determine the optimal solution for her. For *both* of them, in fact."

"Okay. It sounds like you've got a grip on it."

"The things I can get a grip on. But we're dealing with children. Young, vulnerable minds. Ellie's seen and done a lot that she hasn't had time to absorb."

There isn't much to say. We pace in silence.

"How long are you in New Orleans?"

"A few days. As long as you need me, really."

"The FBI is conducting their investigation. I know Tom Morgan. He's good, and we have to help him help us. If you get my meaning."

"You mean help him fill all the holes in his report?"

"Something like that."

I produce a thin smile. "The bad guys on the island were killed with a knife and four different weapon systems. Sheriff Kennedy and Des Krainer were killed with the same Smith & Wesson. There's no way to plug holes like that without finding all the weapons."

"And you suggest?"

"File the ballistics, but don't look too hard. It's the bad guys got shot. Depending on what else the FBI finds, you could make it out to be a gang war."

Stein rolls her eyes. "Gee, why didn't I think of that?"

"Look, it might just turn into a gang war. We have no idea what Luka's partners… or investors… are thinking."

We arrive back at Rowan's room.

"Okay. I'll keep you posted on developments." Stein hesitates. "I am wondering about something."

"I'll help if I can."

"Why did you shoot Shelly in the knee?"

I tilt my head toward Rowan's room. "Reason's in there."

22

DAY FOUR - RESURRECTION BAYOU, 1400 HRS

Albertine and I walk east along the shore. In the opposite direction from the place where she and her congregation hold their ceremonies. Not a big deal for her, but a source of ugly memories for me. It's hard for me to reconcile this ordinary-looking girl with the demonic high priestess I watched the other night.

Harder still to explain is the powerful sexual attraction we feel toward each other. It's too simplistic to say I was turned on by her erotic dance. She and I were attracted from the first. Even more inexplicable, when I went to her after the ceremony, I did not feel threatened.

I believe in forces beyond our understanding. Once, in Kunar, my team was exfiling by helo. I was the last man to get on the Black Hawk. Ran under the whirling blades, stared at the promise of safety inside the open door. The door gunner with his minigun scanned the mountainside behind me.

As I was about to mount and pull myself aboard, I heard

a voice in my head. A man's voice, as clear as though he was standing right next to me. "Down," he said.

No hesitation. I dropped to the ground and ate rocks. There was a crack, and a Dragunov bullet splattered into the Black Hawk's side exactly where my head had been a fraction of a second before. The door gunner swung his minigun around and laid hell on the mountainside.

Willing hands hauled me into the helo. The pilot pulled on the collective, and the Black Hawk took off. The door gunner plastered the mountainside with automatic fire. Didn't want Taliban to try for us with RPGs.

A mile out, the door gunner flipped up his visor and stared at me. "What made you drop like that? That should have been one shot, one kill."

If I had told him the truth, he wouldn't have believed me.

While I profess skepticism and keep my thoughts to myself, I do believe there are forces we can't explain.

Like Albertine sending Bastien and Rémy to fetch me from the swamp. How did she know where I'd be on twenty miles of Old US 51? How did she know I was in trouble?

My fingers brush Albertine's, and I take her hand in mine. Her fingers are thin and delicate. She squeezes gently, and I squeeze back.

"Will you remain in New Orleans long?" Albertine asks.

"A few days. Long enough for the FBI to debrief me."

Albertine lifts her face to me.

"Don't worry," I tell her. "I'm not telling them anything about you, Bastien and Rémy."

"They told me you said they were never on the island."

"That's right. They took their boat with them. The FBI will find that Luka's hitters were killed with bullets from four different firearms. At least one of them with a hand-loaded .43 Spanish."

Bastien's rifle still intrigues me. I may go looking for one, though I'll probably load with smokeless powder. That'll be fun, but could take some work. Maybe I'll spend some time in Montana.

I stop and meet Albertine's eyes. "I *could* stay longer. Do you want me to?"

Albertine gazes at me with sad eyes, reaches for my face. "What you and I want isn't important anymore, Breed."

"What do you mean?"

"*Oshun* says we are not for each other."

I'm open-minded, but this is too much. "What does *Oshun* have to say about it?"

"You will be freed from your dream."

"This is the deal you made with *Oshun*?"

Albertine nods. "And she, with *Legba*."

I want to explode.

"Breed, she told me something I *can* share with you."

"What's that?"

"*Oshun* said 'the boy needs you.'"

My frustration disappears in an instant, replaced by puzzlement. "What boy?"

"I don't know, Breed. She said *you* will know."

"I know him?"

Albertine shakes her head. "Either you know him, or you will meet him. I don't know any more than that."

"Great. Everything with you is a puzzle."

"Is that so bad?" Albertine leans against me. Wiggles her hips until I respond.

"I guess not."

"*Oshun* didn't say we couldn't have a few days together."

THE END

ACKNOWLEDGMENTS

This novel would not have been possible without the support, encouragement, and guidance of my agent, Ivan Mulcahy, of MMB Creative. I would also like to thank my publishers, Brian Lynch and Garret Ryan of Inkubator Books for seeing the novel's potential. The novel benefitted from the feedback of my writing group and Beta readers. Thanks also go to Claire Milto of Inkubator Books for her support in the novel's launch.

If you could spend a moment to write an honest review, no matter how short, I would be extremely grateful. They really do help readers discover my books.

Feel free to contact me at cameron.curtis545@gmail.com. I'd love to hear from you.

ALSO BY CAMERON CURTIS

DANGER CLOSE

(Breed Book #1)

OPEN SEASON

(Breed Book #2)

TARGET DECK

(Breed Book #3)

CLOSE QUARTERS

(Breed Book #4)

BROKEN ARROW

(Breed Book #5)

WHITE SPIDER

(Breed Book #6)

BLACK SUN

(Breed Book #7)

HARD CONTACT

(Breed Book #8)

BLOOD SPORT

(Breed Book #9)

BLOWBACK

(Breed Book #10)

DEATH HUNT

(Breed Book #11)

Breed Thrillers Box Set (Books 1 - 4)